A CARD
NOT PLAYED

A CARD NOT PLAYED

DENNIS JUNG

CITIOFBOOKS, INC.
3736 Eubank NE Suite A1
Albuquerque, NM 87111-3579
www.citiofbooks.com
Hotline: 1 (877) 389-2759
Fax: 1 (505) 930-7244

Ordering Information:
Quantity sales. Special discounts are available on quantity purchases by corporations, associations, and others. For details, contact the publisher at the address above.

Printed in the United States of America.

ISBN-13:	Softcover	979-8-89391-519-8
	Hardcover	979-8-89391-518-1
	eBook	979-8-89391-520-4

Library of Congress Control Number: 2025901472

Table of Contents

OTHR BOOKS BY THE AUTHOIR

Potions (The Eye of God)

The Morning of the World

Still Life In A Red Dress

Jack of All Trades

The Language of the Dead

Signs of Life

The Angel's Chair

States of Exile

The Siren's Refrain

The Uneven Surface of the Soul

A Lightered Shade of Gray

Dedicated to those ones who are brave and resilient enough to practice artifice while remaining true to their heart.

ACKNOWLEDGEMENTS

Again the usual suspects. My dear wife Kathleen for her support and insight into the human psyche. I wish to thank my sister Katie and my brother Steve for their encouragement and support. And finally to Meg for her valuable critique.

FOREWORD

I guess I just can't wash her out of my hair. I'm referring to Lilly DeFranco, of course. I realized after writing THE UNEVEN URFACE OF THE SOUL, the first installment in this series that I wouldn't be able to allow her to slip off stage without a second act. Or a third act it seems. I had to see her through her evolution from outlaw to a semblance of an authentic life, if working as the personal courier for a Mexico City crime boss can be deemed authentic. And all the while the one constant is that she remains a dangerous woman and a captivating one at that. And so we are in the third installment of her saga. The acts and settings may change, but the music remains the same.

I have always been drawn to complicated women. Some cynic might argue that all women are complicated. And my rejoinder would be that complicated doesn't necessarily translate to captivating. Complicated might conjure up attributes such as mercurial, dangerously alluring, unpredictable, challenging, obstinate as hell. But captivating is a wholly different creature. I imagine that one might argue that all or most of those aforementioned traits are the very ones that render a woman captivating. All being parts of the sum. And on second thought, they might be right.

In this third act, the complicated and captivating Lilly DeFranco again finds herself held in the confidence and employ of the crime boss Jeronimo Hermosa. As this story opens, she is serving in the unlikely role of supervising an agave harvest on the behalf of Hermosa's efforts to divest himself of his criminal enterprises. An unexpected encounter with someone from her past leads to her involvement in web of vengeance and subterfuge, which forces her to once again draw on dormant talents and risk not only her own life, but of the people she most cares about.

I set part of a previous novel (THE ANGEL'S CHAIR) in Austin, Texas, a city I once called home for almost twenty-five years and knew intimately. Needless to say, it's the not the same city. In some respects, it is difficult absorb its new vibe now that I am only an occasional visitor. I suspect that more than a few long time residents, especially those that lived there during the golden decade of the nineteen seventies , nowadays suffer fits of nostalgia for the old Austin – the lazy Sunday afternoons at Hippy Hollow, the free concerts at Zilker Park, paying the then outrageous sum of twenty-five dollars to see Van Morrison play at the Armadillo World Headquarters, the laid back vibe of Barton Springs, and so on. Alas, no place remains the same. And yes, the music and restaurant scene, the endless outlets for distraction no doubt appeal to the hordes of California transplants, the techies and entrepreneurs, and seekers of the bright lights of such a unique and vibrant city. But still…

I wanted to remove this story from Mexico as much as I could and place it Stateside. I could have used anyplace, but chose Austin partially out of familiarity, but also because it suited the story line. The city serves as more of a backdrop, a minor character if you will. Who knows, I may choose to revisit it in more depth in a future story.

And speaking of future stories, I have already started on the fourth installment of Lilly DeFranco's journey. Stay tuned.

Santa Fe

December 2024

"Trust everybody, but still cut the cards."

-Finley Peter Dunne

Chapter 1
Jalisco, Mexico

March 2025

It was approaching noon before Lilly DeFranco finally ventured out onto the casita's porch. It had rained during the night and the warm, humid air still smelled of ozone and the flinty, limestone earth. She cinched her silk dressing gown more tightly around her waist as she gazed out across the rolling, corrugated plain stretching into the near distance. The neat rows of spiky, gray-blue agave seemed to undulate like waves in the midday heat.

She flipped open her sunglasses, and before slipping them on, took a cautious sip of her coffee. It was strong and black, just as she preferred it. A decent cup of coffee was one of two things she missed the most while in the prison in Arizona where the coffee was little more than brown water. The other thing she missed was a decent over easy fried egg. Right now neither of them sounded even remotely appealing.

She had felt nauseated for three days, her general lack of appetite aggravated by this morning's spate of vomiting. She explained it away as being due to the *cabrito* stew Jesus, the plantation overseer, had graciously offered her three days ago. At least, she thought it might be the goat meat, although the neat might have just as well been rabbit or ground squirrel. She disliked cooking, so leftovers tended to linger longer than their use by date. She would have to go back to her staple diet of fresh tortillas, bananas, avocados, and whatever she could scrounge from the local *Mercado.* But she vowed to pass on the surprise meat in the future.

She had stayed up until almost three am the night before reading an Elmore Leonard novel– the one about the sexy, quick on the draw US Marshal. It made her think of Harlan Quist, the ex-ATF agent and her one time lover who had once saved her life. She managed to discover he lived on the coast of Oaxaca, but she would never make the effort to seek him out. That had been a different life. One she had no desire to revisit for it was tainted by shame, violence, and retribution.

She took another sip of her coffee as she watched the handful of workers toiling in the neat rows of agave. Most of the plants wouldn't be flowering for at least another couple of weeks. She had learned that the timing of the harvest was critical. Too early or too late could result in a lower yield or an inferior end product.

Jesus, the workers' overseer, was an elderly Zapotec farmer from Oaxaca who the managers and the workers only referred to as *El Viejo.* His counsel as to the exact timing of harvest seemed to vary from day by day depending on not only the agaves' budding blossoms, but also the vagaries of the weather and certain enigmatic celestial alignments that he without fail consulted each evening.

Lilly, along with the old man and the young overseer of the adjoining distillery, had spent the past two weeks negotiating with a labor contractor to hire the required number of workers requited to harvest the *piña.* Now all that remained for Lilly to still accomplish before returning to Mexico City was to review the anticipated production quotas, something she knew absolutely nothing about.

She suspected the real reason her boss sent her here was to render an opinion about Abraham, the brash, young, college-educated manager of the distillery. Abraham had been selected by one of the distillery's silent partners, in this case, a well-known Hollywood actor. Lilly's boss, Jeronimo Hermosa was under the impression the two men's relationship was more than just professional. If such was the case, Lilly had not been able to confirm or discount his suspicions.

She was more than ready to return home, for she missed her life in the bustling urban scene of Mexico City, her expanding circle of newfound friends, and, of course, her lover Jaime.

He had called her the night before to say he would be stopping over for one night before flying to Austin, Texas to deal with some labor troubles at their boos Jeronimo Hermosa's latest hotel acquisition.

Hermosa had once held an esteemed status in the hierarchy of Mexico City's criminal pantheon. The scion of a wealthy and prominent Mexico City family, he had been sent to Texas for his education, even going so far as to earn a graduate degree in business from the University of Texas. Upon his return, he found his niche catering to the burgeoning appetite among the city's nouveau riche for gambling and nightlife.

His first self-made fortune came to fruition by investing in risky and quasi-legitimate real estate deals, his profits then plowed into purchases of nightclubs. From there, he bought interests in casinos. It all came too easily, and before he knew it, he found it even more lucrative to dabble in influence peddling and bribery of public officials. Money laundering became the next natural progression. Soon any form of graft that did not involve drugs or prostitution was on the table. Even though he possessed a strict, almost Puritan moral code, it did not preclude him from resorting to the occasional use of strong arm tactics to achieve his goals.

But those days were long past, and now at the age of seventy-six, Hermosa was divesting himself of his illicit businesses and investing instead in a host of legitimate enterprises. The tequila distillery was just one of his many new acquisitions. To this end, Lilly served as his personal courier and liaison in these new ventures.

She herself had undertaken her own metamorphoses by shedding her own criminal past in the hope of rebuilding a new life. Gone was an identity that included two prison terms, an ill-fated career in armed robbery, and several months on the run from both the US authorities and the Sinaloa cartel.

Jeronimo Hermosa had become her savior, providing her with a job, a new false identity, and the opportunity to regain a sense of self. She was now Lilia Montez, a confidante and personal messenger for one of the few men in Mexico who offered her protection.

She continued scanning the agave fields for a moment longer as she sipped her coffee. She was just about to turn and go back inside when she caught sight of a vehicle speeding down the muddy road leading from the field's entrance. She picked up a pair of binoculars from the porch's railing to see who it might be. If it was Jaime, he was early, she thought with guilty pleasure. They hadn't seen each other in a week, and now the prospect of his companionship lightened her mood.

Peering through the binoculars, she could now see the vehicle was a large sedan, not the four wheel drive SUV Jaime usually rented in Guadalajara. She watched for a moment longer as the sedan turned onto the road leading in the direction of the casita. She saw it was a large, expensive-looking Mercedes sedan that rolled like a rowboat on a rough sea as it maneuvered along the uneven road. The car slowed for a moment as it approached the drive to the casita before turning in.

At first, Lilly thought it might be an unexpected visit from Jeronimo, but quickly realized this would be out of character for him to show up unannounced.

The sedan pulled to a stop at the path leading to the porch. A moment later, a tall, well built man dressed in khaki slacks and a red *guayabera* dismounted from the passenger side, followed by another man exiting from the driver's side. The second man was short and pudgy and wore jeans and a long-sleeved white dress shirt. The taller of the two men, took a moment to survey his surroundings before making his way casually up the path, the shorter man in tow.

As they drew near, Lilly briefly entertained the thought that she had seen the shorter of the two men somewhere once before, an impression that only grew as the two men paused at the foot of the steps. The short one gazed up at her for a moment before removing his sunglasses.

She took in a sudden involuntary breath as the recognition struck her like a slap in the face. Her first instinct was to turn and go inside, but to what end? If they had come for her, there would be no escape.

"Buenos Dias, Señorita," the tall one said with a smile. Unlike his companion, he made no effort to remove his sunglasses.

He had a handsome, well-sculpted face with a broad mouth and white even teeth. His carefully coiffed black hair glistened in the midday sun.

"Buenos Dias," she managed to reply, crossing her arms across her chest, her eyes returning to the short man who gave her a curious look before also smiling. He was bald with a pale, almost pasty complexion. His eyes were as small and round as bullet holes. A thick, black mustache barely concealed his fleshy lips.

The last time she had seen him had been at a dinner party in Culiacan. Estevan, her lover at the time, had introduced them. The encounter had been brief and forgettable. Yet here he was standing on the steps of the porch.

As a precaution, she had changed her appearance soon after she found herself traveling around Mexico on Jeronimo's behalf. She had dyed her auburn hair a dark brown and wore it in a long braid. A plastic surgeon had re-sculpted her nose that had been broken by a cartel thug. She had also replaced her reading glasses with dark brown-tinted contacts that concealed her blue eyes. Even though she doubted the man would recognize her, she couldn't discount the possibility someone had given her up.

She offered them each a nervous smile. "Can I help you?" she asked. "I'm sorry, but I don't speak a whole lotta Spanish," she added in an exaggerated Southern drawl.

"I was told at the gate that you are the representative of the owner," the tall one said in heavily-accented English.

"Oh no. I am only one of the botanists. *Una botánica.* Did I say that right? I was hired as a consultant."

"Una botánica." He stared at her for a moment before going on. "I was hoping there might be someone who could place me in touch with the owner of your operation. *Señor* Hermosa, yes?"

"I don't know that name, but I've only been here a coupla weeks. All I know is my paycheck comes from a corporation in Guadalajara. *Nectar Azul.* I do know that one of the owners is some Hollywood movie star. I haven't had the pleasure of making his acquaintance yet," she said with a playful shrug. "I tell you what I do have is an email address for their office if that helps."

He gave her a look that telegraphed his skepticism. "That is very strange for my sources tell me that *Señor* Hermosa was here several days ago to attend a meeting with a *Señor* Morales."

Lilly fumbled for an answer. "I'm sorry, but that comes as news to me. I've been busy here in the fields. I guess maybe I could've missed them. Or maybe they were meeting in Guadalajara."

"Perhaps, one of the field workers has seen him," the short one offered.

"Oh, I doubt it. I'm with them all the time."

"Pero hoy no hay trabajo."

She gave him a blank look, knowing full well he was trying to trip her up and see if she understood Spanish.

"You do no work today?" he asked, perhaps reading her confusion.

"Oh." She clutched her stomach. *"Mi... estómago.* Sick, yes? I tell you what. Do you have a card? You know, just in case this *Señor...* What was his name again?"

"Hermosa," the short one replied with obvious annoyance.

"Yeah. In case he shows up I can give him your card."

"No necesauo," he said, his eyes never leaving hers.

"Or your name maybe in case he asks?"

The short one seemed to think about it for a moment before reaching into his shirt pocket, retrieving a card and extending it to her.

She took the card and read the two words printed on it. *Empresas Marigold,* and below it was a phone number. She turned it over, but the reverse side was blank.

"Señor Hermosa will know who we represent," the tall one said offering her a wide smile. He nodded and turned to walk away.

The short on lingered as he studied her. Had he finally recognized her?

"And your name, *señorita?"* he asked after a long, uncomfortable moment.

"Gloria. I'd offer you two gentlemen a cold drink, but I'm outta ice," she added.

The machete she kept for killing snakes hung on a hook just inside the door. If he gave just the slightest inkling of remembering her, she would invite him in. Then what? Hack him to death? And what about the other one? Would it be worth the risk? She just hoped it wouldn't come to that, for she had no intention of running again.

"No gracias." He smiled before turning and joining his companion.

"Assholes" she muttered softly as she watched them get in the car. There had been a time when she had fed the short guy's boss to the pigs at a farm outside of Culiácan. Another life. No pigs here, she thought, allowing herself a smile. She felt confident he hadn't recognized her. Either that or he had been yet unable to place where he knew her from.

She looked at the card again. Marigold Enterprises. But no name or even a phone number. It seemed strange, cartel gangsters using business cards. What was next? Their own website? Facebook? If she could take a guess, these two were bent on muscling in on Hermosa's tequila business. The word was the cartels were buying up agave fields and distilleries, or worse yet, simply expropriating them. She had even broached the subject with Jeronimo, warning him of the risk, but he seemed unconcerned.

As she watched them drive off, the short guy's name suddenly occurred to her. It was Gustavo something. Back in the day, he used to be with the Sinaloa cartel, but this was the Jalisco cartel's territory. Had he changed teams?

She wondered where the two men would've gotten the impression Jeronimo had been here the previous week for some kind of meeting. It didn't make sense. As soon as she got back to Mexico City, she would report this to Jeronimo. His reaction would undoubtedly prove interesting.

She tossed the cold dregs of her coffee over the porch railing and went inside.

Chapter 2

Jaime had called earlier that afternoon to let her know it would be close to five before he would arrive, but here it was five-thirty and still no sign of him. Lilly propped her bare feet onto the railing, opened another can of *limonada*, and was just about to call him when she spotted an SUV approaching the cutoff to the casita.

She had grown used to his tardiness although it continued to be a source of irritation since they first became involved a year ago. Still, it certainly hadn't proven to be a deal breaker. They first became involved when Jeronimo had tasked them with extracting his granddaughter from an unsavory situation in Houston.

Jaime had once been a homicide detective in San Antonio, Texas before finding his way into Jeronimo's employ as a troubleshooter. Jaime liked to think of himself more as Jeronimo's Human Resources administrator in charge of hiring and firing he would explain with appropriate sarcasm.

There had been a time when Lilly had been resigned to the unlikelihood of any reawakening of intimacy in her life.

The possibility of romance had been cast away like most of the detritus of her past life. Then Jaime had stumbled into her path and she hadn't looked back.

Their relationship was comfortable and easy with a healthy degree of day to day, month to month commitment that seemed to work for the both of them. Still, she had a depth of feelings for him that she resisted admitting to herself much less to Jaime. Was that love? For most of her life, any form of commitment approaching that four letter word had simply never been on her radar.

She rose to her feet to wait for him. The first thing she noticed when he started up the path was the absence of an overnight bag. In place of his usual jeans and a T-shirt, he wore dark blue dress slacks and a long-sleeved white shirt with the sleeves rolled up.

"Hey *güero,*" she greeted him, using an endearment for a blonde-haired Hispanic.

He bounded up the stairs and took her into his arms. They kissed until both of them were forced to come up for air. He let her go and stepped back.

"I'm hoping you dressed up like this on my account," he said as he took note of her sheer silk dressing gown. It was quite obvious that she wore nothing underneath.

"No work today and I haven't felt up to getting dressed. I did take a long bath though. Smell," she said, offering him her arm. "It's that bath oil you bought me."

He brought her arm up to his nose and held it there a moment. She reached up and ran her fingers through his thick blonde hair. He had a smooth, tanned complexion that made him look younger than his forty years. Only the fine delta of wrinkles around his eyes betrayed his age.

He offered her a quick smile and reached up for her hand. She studied him. There was something in his eyes that hinted at something more than mere fatigue.

"You're not sleeping, are you? She asked, eying him closely.

"I'm sorry I'm late," he replied, ignoring her question. "The thing is ..." he started to say, averting his eyes. "I can't stay."

"What do you mean you can't stay? You told me…"

He pressed his fingers to her lips. "I know. But I have to be in Austin first thing in the morning. It couldn't he helped."

"You were just there two weeks ago. What gives?"

"The same job I told you about."

"Jeronimo's fancy boutique hotel?"

"Yeah, it's got staffing issue. People quitting left and right, and plumbing problems. That's what happens when you buy a place that's ninety years old. It's a money pit. That first trip was just to scope things out. Now I have to deal with it," he said, running his index finger across his mouth.

An unconscious mannerism like that was what was known as a tell, a subtle and involuntary move that signaled evasiveness, if not an outright lie. She knew him well enough by now to know when he wasn't being entirely honest with her. He must not be much of gambler, she had thought on more than one occasion.

"Okay. So why don't I come with you? I could…"

"No," he replied, cutting her off. "Not this trip."

"Goddamn Jeronimo," she murmured and shook her head.

He shrugged. "It's something that can't wait. So when do you go back?" he asked. It seemed obvious that he wanted to change the subject.

She took a swallow of her *limonada* before replying. "I go back the day after tomorrow. Gordon, the asshole actor, is flying in tomorrow and wants a briefing."

She slumped back into her chair.

"Don't pout," he said, squatting down in front of her and taking her hands in his.

"I'm allowed to pout. If you don't like it, then do something about it."

"Well, do you have any half and half?" he asked, taking her can of *limonada* from her and taking a sip. Half and half was their private joke and an offhand reference to a certain sex act.

"Matter of fact, I do. You'd better come inside and make sure it hasn't gone bad," she replied, getting to her feet and turning to go inside without bothering to look back at him.

Chapter 3

The casita was a simple one room affair that had been built to house a shepherd back before the property had been turned into an agave plantation. The small, utilitarian bathroom had only been added on in the past year. An ancient, rusty refrigerator, a small chipped porcelain sink and a hot plate comprised the kitchen. Two long cracks marked the stained cement floor. The only furnishings were a rickety wooden table, two ratty lawn chairs, and a single bed with what Lilly called a prison mattress. Little wonder Jaime wasn't keen on spending the night.

"Are you still mad?" Jaime asked, scooting close to avoid falling out of the bed.

"Sure am." She craned her neck and bit him on the lip.

"Christ, Lilly! That hurt."

"Good. I warned you I was a biter. So are you going to tell me about what exactly you're doing in Austin that can't wait a day? It's no business of mine if you've got a lover there."

"Hey. Where in the hell is this coming from? I told you. It's business," he said, pulling away to look at her.

"What kind of business?"

"I told you. It's just some bullshit labor dispute. You know, Human Resources stuff," he said in an obvious attempt to make light of it. "What's wrong? I can tell something's eating you."

She rolled out if bed and slipped on her gown. "Two guys came by here today," she said, turning to look at him. "They wanted to get in touch with Jeronimo."

"Oh yeah? Who was it?"

"They didn't really say, but I recognized one of them. If I recall correctly, he used to be a mid-level errand boy for the Sinaloa cartel. Gustavo something."

"Wait. You know him?"

"I met him once at a party in Culiacán."

"Did he remember you?" he asked, sitting up in bed, his interest obviously piqued.

"I'm not sure. I don't think so. What was odd was that they were under the impression Jeronimo was here this week for a meeting. Do you know anything about that?"

"No. I sure don't," he said, running his finger across his mouth again.

"They thought he was here meeting with someone named Morales."

Jaime grunted. "I don't know anyone by that name. I need to take a shower," he said, abruptly getting up and disappearing into the bathroom.

"You do that," she muttered under her breath. She wasn't stupid. The fact he hadn't commented further or asked more told her there was something he wasn't telling her. His evasiveness and the sour taste in her mouth from her memories of Culiacán had put her on edge.

She went into the kitchen and took out some cheese, a plate of fruit, and a bowl of guacamole from the refrigerator. There was no way he was getting a meal out of this, she thought, struggling to overcome her irritation.

When fifteen minutes later, he emerged from his shower and back in his street clothes, she could tell he was still uncharacteristically distant, as if distracted.

"What's going on, Jaime?"

He shook his head. "I can't…." He turned and took a beer from the refrigerator.

"Can't what?"

"It's just business that Jeronimo doesn't want me discussing with anyone. You never travel to the States, so you're out of the loop," he said with obvious irritation

She stared at him for a moment before getting up and making her way to the sink. "Okay. So when do you get back?" she asked, as she pretended to wash her breakfast dishes

"I can't say. A few days at most."

She came back to the table, and they sat staring at each for a long moment.

"You know I'll get Jeronimo to tell me," she said.

He shrugged. "There's nothing to tell. Look can we drop it?"

"Sure." She managed a smile. "Eat."

They nibbled on the cheese, mango slices, tortilla chips, and the bowl of guacamole, all the while engaging in small talk about the distillery, gossip about the actor partner and his suspected liaison with Abraham, and tidbits of news about their mutual friends back in Mexico City.

When it came time for him to leave, he took her in his arms and held her for what seemed longer than necessary. He kissed her softly on the lips and told her he would catch up with her back in Mexico City in a few days.

"You call me as soon as you get to Austin," she said, stroking his face.

He nodded. "Will do. Love you."

"I love you, too. Be careful."

He walked off, waving over his shoulder without turning. As she watched him drive off, her instincts told her his mood and reticence to talk about what he was doing in Austin could only mean there was something waiting there other than a simple labor dispute. Another woman? No, that just wasn't him. Something dodgy? Maybe. He never had been the type to disclose all he did for Jeronimo, she thought as she lingered on the porch. It also bothered her that he seemed to take such little interest in the Gustavo guy and the bullshit about a meeting. All she knew was that Jeronimo was going to catch hell if he didn't come clean with her.

In the distance, a bank of angry-looking storm clouds promised more rain. Sure enough, she spotted *El Viejo* gazing up at the sky, no doubt searching the darkening sky for omens. Perhaps, she should consult with him regarding the day's events.

She gathered the dressing gown more tightly around her as a gust of cool air stirred the still evening air. She stood there another moment before turning and going back inside.

Chapter 4
AUSTIN-BERGSTROM INTERNATIONAL AIRPORT
The Following Morning

Jaime checked his phone as he stood in the line at Starbucks. The only message was from the Four Seasons welcoming him to Austin and confirming his reservation. There was no message from Jeronimo. Nor had Lilly tried calling. For a moment, he contemplated calling her, but balked at the prospect of having to lie to her anymore. He knew she would be irritated if he didn't at least text her. After another day without hearing from him, she would be past worrying and truly pissed. Hadn't she said she would be returning to Mexico City the day after tomorrow? If so, she would undoubtedly confront Jeronimo and the cat would be out of the bag.

He placed his coffee order with a pimply-faced young woman who avoided eye contact. Something he had wished the immigration agent would have done, who in spite of Jaime's valid US passport had given him the third degree when he noticed the three entry and exit stamps into Columbia. That and the fact Jaime had a stamp indicating his entry back in the Sates the year before but the agent's computer didn't show any evidence of his exit.

He and Lilly had been forced to fly back into Mexico illegally by private plane in the company of Jeronimo's granddaughter Kate who didn't posses a passport much less any other form of identification. There was also the problem of Kate being a wanted fugitive.

He took his Americano and a scone and found an empty table. He always enjoyed scrutinizing his fellow passengers and trying to guess the possible purposes for their travel. Keen observational skills had once served him well during his days as a detective.

A few tables away sat an attractive, well-dressed middle-aged woman who seemed engaged in a heated conversation on her cell phone. He caught snippets of what she was saying. There was something about a lawsuit and adultery. At one point, she looked in his direction and realized he might be eavesdropping on her conversation, and quickly turned away. Was she speaking with a lover, her wayward husband, or maybe just her attorney? There was a story there, he thought, sipping his coffee and turning his attention elsewhere.

He tossed his empty coffee cup in the recycle bin, took his carryon bag and started for the exit, all the while studying passerby's faces. He paused once at a magazine stand to see if he might be being followed. He doubted they would attempt to call him on his phone. So how would they reach out? Would there be a knock on his hotel room door? Or possibly a stranger sidling up to him in the hotel lobby?

It could be anyone. He expected it would be someone Hispanic, but then again they might use a cut out; a nondescript older woman or a teenager carrying a skateboard that they had paid fifty dollars to pass on a message. He had been instructed to wait at the hotel and someone would contact him.

He made his way out of the terminal and stepped out into the warm humid air. It was only March and the temperature felt near ninety. He started to cross the street in the direction of the car rental kiosks when a bulky Hispanic man in an ill-fitting suit and smoking a cigarette started walking beside him.

"Señor Soledad. Sígame, por favor," he said softly without looking at him.

At the same time, a newer model, black Toyota Land Cruiser pulled up to the curb. The man nodded with his chin, gesturing to Jaime that his ride had arrived. Jaime took a glance around before stepping toward the open rear door. If there was some sort of surveillance he doubted it would be easy to spot.

He could only assume the DEA or the local police intelligence unit had eyes on the SUV. He imagined that within a couple of hours someone would be analyzing his photo. Would they figure out his identity? Jaime Soledad, a cashiered ex-homicide detective from San Antonio. When they checked and saw that he had arrived on a flight from Guadalajara, they would probably reach out to their counterparts in the Mexican Federal Police and discover that they were looking at a member of the Jeronimo Hermosa crime family of Mexico City. The intelligence file would reveal that the organization was small and rather inconsequential, a shadow of its former self; a mere a footnote in the record of Mexican criminal enterprises. Still, they would wonder why a member of Hermosa's organization had climbed into a SUV believed to belong to a capo in the Jalisco cartel.

The man in the ill-fitting suit held open the door and Jaime crawled in the back. The man then closed the door and walked away. Jaime glanced over at his fellow passenger, an attractive woman in a dark blue business suit. She wore her black hair twisted into a tight chignon. A pair of oversized and darkly tinted sunglasses obscured her eyes and most of her face. She glanced at Jaime, her bright red lips curling into a discrete smile.

"*Bienvendo a Austin,* Jaime. I will be escorting you to your hotel," she added in a husky and slightly-accented voice.

He nodded, and as the SUV slid into traffic, he glanced once more to the street behind them. And so it begins, he thought to himself.

Chapter 5
MEXICO CITY
Two Days Later

It was late afternoon by the time Hilario, Jeronimo's chauffer, pulled into the circular driveway in front of Jeronimo Hermosa's mansion. As was Hilario's time-honored routine, the old man meticulously switched off the ignition, nodded at Lilly in the rear view mirror to acknowledge their arrival, and then slowly and laboriously dismounted with an unhurried grace consistent with his advanced years. As was also his custom, the old man wore the same baggy black suit with wide lapels that was shiny with wear. Before opening her door, he meticulously brushed the lapels of the suit with a small brush. Jeronimo once speculated to Lilly that the suit most likely predated his own birth.

In contrast to his wrinkled, tobacco-colored face, Hilario's hair remained thick and coal black. He wore it long and pulled back into a braided and tightly coiled ponytail.

Lilly waited as Hilario completed this tedious routine. The simple act of her humoring his ritual had resulted in a convivial, almost intimate relationship between the two of them.

"Señorita," he croaked and offered a curt bow.

"Gracias, Hilario," she replied, taking his proffered hand and stepping from the car.

She took only a moment to survey the estate's well-manicured lawn and gardens as her mind was focused on other matters, primarily the reason Jaime had never called her or responded to her calls.

It was only when the gardener, an elderly Indio in overalls offered her a salutation that she stopped to look around and smile, feeling it rude to fail to acknowledge and admire the gardener's work.

The mansion was situated in the Miguel Hidalgo neighborhood and bordered the Bosque De Chapultepec. From the sidewalk, a break in the tall conifer trees allowed a view of the looming edifice of the Chapultepec Castle.

Jeronimo had inherited the house from his parents and had done little to alter the gardens or the mansion's imposing, neo-colonial exterior. His father had been a prominent banker who had also owned a large sisal plantation in the Yucatan that he had inherited from his own father, the later sale of which financed Jeronimo's stake in a pair of Mexican casinos. This had been his first foray into the world outside his father's staid, respectable business world. Now it seemed Jeronimo had come full circle as he attempted to reform his image as a crime boss and become a respectable businessman.

As she approached the stairs onto the portico, a lean, young man in a dark business suit and striped tie stepped from the shadows and motioned for her to stop. Slung over his shoulder was what appeared to be an Uzi. She was surprised because the usual guardian of the gates was a grizzled, older gentleman by the name of Alphonso who usually left his antiquated shot gun propped casually against a nearby potted fig. Before she could inquire as to Alphionso's absence, the young man retrieved a cell phone from his jacket pocket and punched in a number.

"Dile que Lilia está aquí," she said, offering him a look of cool authority. She turned to survey the portico. At the far end, she saw another man in similar attire standing in the shadows and also carrying some sort of automatic weapon. What was going on, she thought as the guard relayed what she had said. A few seconds passed before he palmed his phone and nodded with his head for her to enter.

She was equally surprised when the maid Maria failed to open the door and welcome her as was her usual custom. Lilly hesitated a moment and strode quickly down the long, wide hallway, her running shoes squeaking on the highly polished marble floor.

Unlike the mansion's more traditional exterior, Jeronimo had chosen to refurbish the interior walls in teak and accented with mosaics of vibrantly painted ceramic and glass tiles. The only other décor were a series of basalt carvings of Aztec deities.

For once, she didn't pause to whistle to the finches flitting in the half-dozen or so cages lining the wall. Nor did she stop to exchange banter with Bruno, the scarlet macaws perched on a bare tree branch.

She stopped outside the door to Jeronimo's office in an attempt to compose herself and reel in her anger. She knocked, but didn't wait for an invitation to enter.

"What the fuck, Jeronimo?" she spurted out, her outburst surprising her as much as it did the older man sitting behind the desk. She wasted no time in stepping around the large leather sofa and stopping in front of his desk with her arms crossed in obvious indignation.

The wall behind Jeronimo consisted of several immense glass sliding doors that opened on to a large solarium, its dominant feature a twenty-foot-high wall of black lava studded with dozens of orchids and stag horn ferns. The study itself was rather Spartan, its few furnishings consisting of a leather and teak sofa, a large Afghan Kilim, and a glass-topped desk the size of a large dining table.

Seemingly not offended by her outburst, Jeronimo raised one hand in an attempt to calm her. "*Cálmate chica.*"

He had a longish, fine-boned face beneath a stylishly coiffed mane of silver hair. His mouth was wide and generous with thin, aristocratic lips that rarely gifted a smile. Only his deep- set hazel eyes ever revealed any hint of emotion. They now reflected a mixture of mild rebuke and weariness.

"Where's Jaime? He never called me when he got to Austin. It's not like him to not call me. Is he two timing me? If so, you'd better tell me."

"Two timing? *¿Qié es eso?*"

"You've talked to him, haven't you?"

Jeronimo cleared his throat. "I understand you had visitors."

She glared at him in confusion. "What? Don't change the subject. Wait. How did you know about that?"

"Jaime called me from the airport in Guadalajara. I believe this was one of your visitors," he said, leaning forward and swiveling the computer monitor around so she could see it.

She leaned closer to study the image. It was obviously a police mug shot that showed a jowly, bald man with a bushy black mustache. Written in chalk on the placard draped around his neck was the name Gustavo Encinas Ybarra.

"Yeah, that's him. What's going on?"

"This man was once with the Sinaloa."

"Yeah, I knew that. I met him once in Culiácan. You said he used to be with Sinaloa. Who does he play for now and why is he showing up at the plantation asking about some meeting you had there last week?"

Jeronimo held up his finger. "And this man was with him?" he said, clicking the keyboard.

The image appeared to be a photograph taken at some social function gauging from the host of well dressed subjects surrounding a tall man wearing a white suit and holding a champagne flute in one hand. He looked younger, but it was the same man. Back at the plantation, his eyes had been concealed by his sunglasses, but now she saw they were deep-set and pale. An attractive young woman in an evening gown had her arm draped over his shoulder.

"That's him alright. Who is he?"

"He uses the name Miguel Becerra. He is a capo with the Jalisco New Generation."

"I knew they were cartel assholes. They've got eyes on your distillery, don't they? I told you they would be making a move on you. You're not dealing with those people, are you?"

He didn't reply, but instead turned the computer monitor back around to face him.

"This has something to do with Jaime going to Austin, doesn't it?" she asked.

Jeronimo offered her a wan smile. "You never fail to impress me, Lilia. Nothing escapes you. It is one of the reasons I trust you with my business."

"Quit the bullshit and cut to the chase, *jefe*. What's Jaime doing?"

He stared at her for a moment before reaching down and retrieving a crystal decanter of brown liquor from a drawer. He produced a pair of matching tumblers and poured in a couple of fingers worth into each glass.

"*No gracias,*" she said as he offered her one of the tumblers. "*Mi estomago* is already shot to hell."

He nodded and slumped back in his chair before going on. "This is no business of yours," he said softly.

"It's some kind of hostile takeover, isn't? That's the reason you've got those two *pistoleros* on the porch."

"*Dios! Basta de preguntas.*" he said with a hint of irritation. He took a sip of his tequila and shook his head. "Very well, you have a right to know, but I must tell you again that you will have no part in this. It is for your own good."

"I don't need protecting. You of all people should know that."

"Yes." He allowed himself a smile of amusement. "You are dangerous in your own right. But this is a delicate situation. And you are too invested. You and Jaime. I cannot allow your feelings for each other to complicate things."

She started to object, knowing full well when it was best to wait him out. It was odd that this was one of the few times he made mention of she and Jaime's relationship.

He seemed to be deliberating what to say next, his hands clasped together. "There is a reason he has not called you," he said with a hint of a smile. "You see, it is to appear that Jaime is betraying me,"

Chapter 6

Lilly stared at Jeronimo, her mouth agape.

"What? I don't understand. What are you saying?"

"Lilia. Please," he said, raising his hands. "Allow me to explain."

"You're damn right you're going to explain. You're asking Jaime to act like he's screwing you over?"

"Precisely."

"But why?"

He studied her a moment as if editing in his mind what he was about to say. He settled back in his chair and took a sip of his tequila.

"Eight years ago, I was forced to deal with a situation in a manner that I am not proud of. You must understand that things were different then. I was different. I had many pressures. *Distraciones.*" He paused before going on.

"This thing I did was a matter of honor, you see. But I found it necessary to set an example. And to distance myself from… certain elements. You are well aware that I will have no part in drug trafficking or prostitution. Or the weapons trade for that matter. I am not… I refuse to become like the cartels. You know this."

He paused again to take a sip of his tequila.

"There was an individual, a man who I treated as one of my own. *Como la familia.* ¿Si? I was the best man at his wedding. His wife was my cousin twice removed. I brought him into my business. I even hoped to one day give him a position of great responsibility in my organization. To my regret, I misjudged him. This man …He became *avaro*. Greedy, yes? And he betrayed me by dealing narcotics and selling guns to the cartels. I found this out and I…" He waved his hand as if he were dispelling something vile and foul. "As I said it was a matter of honor that required me to do such a thing."

Lilly suddenly realized she knew this story. Jaime had recounted it to her one night in a hotel bar in Houston while explaining how he had first met Jeronimo. At the time of the incident, Jaime was out of a job, having been fired from the police force in San Antonio as a result of a bribery investigation.

Against his better judgment, he had allowed himself to be talked into helping a friend ferry three stolen SUVs to a ranch in Mexico. As fortune would have it, Jaime arrived late to the drop off site only to find his friend and the other smuggler dead, along with several Mexicans. The only men left standing were Jeronimo, his mend, and a man kneeling in the dirt.

It seemed that Jeronimo and his men had arrived too late to save Jaime's friends. However, Jeronimo assured Jaime that he had dealt with the men who were responsible for the murders of his two fellow smugglers. All that remained was deciding the fate of their leader. Jeronimo had offered Jaime the opportunity to exact his revenge, but Jaime declined as he was unwilling to kill an unarmed man.

Jeronimo must have been impressed with what seemed Jaime's sense of honor for later that night on the long drive back to Mexico City offered Jaime a job.

Jaime was never quite sure who had performed the *coup de grace* on the man kneeling in the sand. It was months later after a late night meeting with Jeroinimo over tequilas that the story was revealed.

"I am ashamed to say that I attempted to force Jaime to do something that I myself was not prepared to do."

"Jaime told me," she blurted out.

He looked at her in surprise. "He told you," he said, more as a statement than a question.

"He told me that for a long time he never knew for sure if it was you who executed you're… this guy you were close to."

Jeronimo looked away, his affliction evident in the way he lowered his head.

"Yes, in the heat of the moment, I killed this man who was almost like a son to me. As I said, I am not proud of this. It is easy to say that I was a different man then. Not ruthless, but rigid. What I did has been a wound I have endured ever since. And now, I am being asked to pay the price for this sin."

He again offered her the tumbler of tequila, but she declined with the shake of her head. And again she knew to wait him out. He took a sip of tequila from the glass she had declined before going on.

"This man. Ramón was his name. It seems he had a brother who has finally decided to seek his vengeance. The man who calls himself Miguel Becerra."

"The same Jalisco capo who was at the plantation?"

"*Si.* The very one. His real name is Miguel Ramos."

"And he knows you killed his brother?"

Jeronimo nodded and grew silent for a moment. "One of my men who was there that night has betrayed me," he said finally. "He has cast his lot with Jalisco. He was the one who told Becerra. I have since dealt with him."

"Dealt with him? How? Or should I ask?"

Part of her really didn't want to know. In the rather short time she had been associated with Jeronimo, she had never known him to resort to violence. Yes, he no doubt had underlings who deal with matters that required a heavy hand, but he was surely not like the cartel thugs.

"I did not have him killed if that is what you are thinking. No, we reached an accommodation. He did suffer certain penalties and my assurances of even greater punishment if he failed to cooperate. But instead I turned him. I believe that is the term. He is now my spy within Jalisco. And as such, I instructed him to inform Becerra that there was someone else in my organization that was willing to betray me."

"Jaime. Shit."

Jeronimo nodded. "Becerra does not know that I am aware that he is the brother of the man I executed." He paused again before going on.

"My spy tells me that Becerra is a rising star in the Jalisco. At least, he seems to believe he is."

Her mind raced as she tried to connect the dots – the visit from Becerra and Gustavo Ybarra and their impression that a meeting had occurred between Jeronimo and this Morales.

"Back up. Who is this Morales they thought you were meeting with?"

"Jesus Morales is a Sinaloa capo."

"I'm confused Why would…Wait. So does Becerra think you're making some kind of deal with the Sinaloa? Is that it? What the hell is going on, *jefe*?"

"*Esperar, chica*" he said, holding up his hand. "Allow me to explain. There was no meeting obviously. It was … What is the term? A false flag. To muddy the waters," He paused before going on. "As I said, Miguel Becerra is an ambitious man. There are rumors of a shakeup in the leadership of Jalisco. And Becerra hopes to come out on top"

"I'm still having difficulty following."

"It is…. *muy complicado,*" he replied, setting his tequila a side.

On the streets, Jeronimo Hermsoa was known as El *Zoro Plateado.* The Silver Fox. She knew him well enough to guess he had something up his sleeve.

"You see, I wish to derail his ambitions. To do that I must force his hand," he said finally

"Force his hand? To do what?"

"To kill me, of course. Or to at least try."

Chapter 7

She wasn't sure how to react. She had long ago decided to distance herself from the arcane chicanery and subterfuge of Jeronimo's illicit businesses. Too much of her life had been stained by criminality. What Jeronimo had so far revealed only reinforced these inclinations. All she knew was that somehow Jaime would be mixed up in it.

"I don't like this, jefe. I don't like Jaime getting involved in this."

"Perhaps, he told you that I have had some labor problems at the hotel in Austin. Problems I have discovered that Becerra is behind. You see, it is how he intends to lure me to Austin,"

"So he can kill you there? "

Jeronimo nodded.

"But why in Austin? Why not here?"

"For one thing, I am too well protected here. Secondly, the cartels wish to avoid calling any undue focus on their activities here in the city. In Austin, I can be dealt with quietly without drawing much attention from the authorities or the other carrels."

Before she could say anything, he went on. "There are certain developments unfolding here in the city. Power struggles. Shifting alliances. Both the Sinaloa and the Jalisco cartels are attempting to gain a stronger foothold here. Until recently, La Unión Tepito controlled most things here, but they have splintered. The other cartels see an opportunity to move in. At one time they would have considered me to be either an obstacle or an ally in their efforts. But now they merely see me as a possible… conduit to the levers of power. You see, I still have a great deal of influence with government officials. As you know, I have begun to divest myself of anything remotely illegal. La Union has taken over the majority of my protection business."

Lilly was well aware that at one time one of Jeronimo's main sources of income was the protection rackets. He offered protection to perhaps hundreds of businesses in the city. His rates, if you wanted to call them that, had never been usurious. It had been like an insurance policy for these businesses against theft, bribery, and all other threats. None of them ever complained for they welcomed Jeronimo's protection.

"I still don't see where Jaime fits in all this?"

"Jaime will be my Trojan Horse, as it were. ¿Lo *entiendes?* He will serve his new master by supposedly luring me into his trap. Now it is simply up to me to step into it."

"I can't believe I'm saying this, but why don't you just put out a contract on Becerra? Have him wacked."

"Wacked?"

"You know. Disappear him. I'm sure…"

He held up his hand. "No. That is no longer who I am. You see, I do not have to kill him. I plan instead to have the US authorities eliminate his threat to me."

Chapter 8

A phone call interrupted their conversation. Lilly got the impression it was regarding some travel arrangements for the following day. It gave her some time to digest all that Jeronimo had revealed. It sounded all too complicated. Jeronimo tossed his cell phone aside and stared at his computer monitor, his distraction obvious.

"Are you going to tell me just how you plan on doing this?" she asked after a long moment of silence.

He looked at her as if he had forgotten she was there. "My sources tell me that Becerra is high on the DEA's most wanted list. Drug trafficking is the least of it. He has also been implicated in the attempted assassination of a federal prosecutor."

"And you really think he'll risk going to Austin?"

"Yes, I do. For one thing, his ego and overconfidence will lead him to disregard the risk of traveling to the US. Once he is there, it will only be a matter of securing his location and then notifying the American authorities."

"You know that won't be the end of it. He'll probably know you were the one who ratted him out to the Feds. He'll have one of his people come for you."

"No, that will not happen. My spy tells me Becerra has many enemies in Jalisco who are eager to betray him and be rid of him. What I have not told you is that all of this is the result of extensive negotiations between myself and Jalisco."

"You're making deals with them?"

"I am only forestalling the inevitable. In exchange for certain considerations, Jalisco will guarantee the safety of my family. Kate, you, Jaime and all of my men in exchange for my help in eliminating Becerra."

"Come on, *jefe*. I know these people. You know them. Do you really take them at their word?"

He shrugged.

"I still think you should just have him wacked. I mean that kind of shit happens all the time down here."

"If the Americans take care of him it is less… messy for all involved."

"I still think you're underestimating what could happen. And this plan of yours… I'm sorry, but you're risking the life of someone I care about. Someone I love." There she had openly admitted it.

"I understand. I do, Lilia. If it is any consolation, this wasn't my idea to keep you away. It was Jaime's."

"Shit. That sounds about right. I still don't understand why Austin? It all sounds too complicated. "

"Jalisco and Becerra have established a presence there. The city is becoming a conduit for moving narcotics into the States. It is close to the border. It is a large city with major highways, an international airport, and many places and ways to hide such operations. As far as his choosing Austin to kill me, Becerra believes there will be less exposure and risk for him than if he attempts to deal with me here in Mexico City. So it will seem as if I am going to Austin to check on my interests there and then I will suffer some unfortunate accident."

"*Estas loco.* I mean, what could possibly go wrong? Face it, *jefe.* You're going to need me."

"I promised Jaime I would keep you out of this."

"Screw him. He knows me better than that."

"*Ah, Chica.* I cannot allow that."

"You know if you don't have Jaime to watch your back, then the next best person would be me."

"You told me you no longer wished to receive such assignments. After you rescued Kate, you said *estabas terminasda. No mas.*"

"I know what I said, but this is different, there's an advantage to me being a woman and an American, I'd be a low profile. Plus, you're forgetting I know these people. I know how they think. Look, if nothing else, I can be your… counsel."

Jeronimo clicked his tongue in disapproval, but she sensed that he appeared to be at least considering her proposal.

"Very well," he said after a moment, "but you will remain only in the background."

"*Ojos extra.* Someone to watch your back. You must be taking someone else. A bodyguard."

"I thought Raphael."

"Your nephew? Please. He's not up to something like this. Yeah, I know that he speaks English and spends lots of time in Texas, but…" She bit her tongue. She wanted to say he was a showboat. He was impetuous, full of himself and totally out of his depth for something like this.

"You don't agree?" Jeronimo asked. "Very well, then who would you suggest?"

I don't know, but anyone but Raphael. How about Beto? You've used him before to deal with sketchy situations."

"He doesn't speak English very well."

"Then how about Mateo?"

"His wife is quite ill with cancer he would not leave her bed side."

"So who else is there?"

"*¿Quizás* Ernesto?" he replied.

Lilly shook her head. Ernesto was one of Jeronimo's oldest and most trusted lieutenants. Still, she just didn't see him as right for this.

"I thought you told me once how he was too heavy handed, too old school. I mean he might be great for getting people to cough up their debts, but for something like this?"

"You underestimate him. He has what you like to call street smarts. He may be old and fat, but he is like you. *Astuto. Sí.* He reads things."

"He speaks English?"

Jeronimo shrugged. "Well enough. They will expect a bodyguard, but not you. You will travel separately. And you must promise to stay in the shadows. I will only use you if needed. Understood?"

"Okay, I can do that."

It took her only a moment to sort out not only her motivations, but also her allegiances - Jaime, for sure. And Jeronimo? He was family, almost like the father she never had. She wouldn't hesitate to risk her own life to protect either of them.

Jeronimo glanced at his watch. "You will stay for dinner? Maria promises *Pescado Zarandeado. Y flan naranjo.*"

"I think I'll pass. I'm not really hungry. Besides, I need to drop by Kate's and tell her to water my plants."

"Give her my love. And tell her to come see me. We leave in the morning. I will book your flight and have Hilario pick you up and bring you to the airport."

"That's probably not a good idea. You know. I stay in the shadows. I'll see you in the morning" she said, getting to her feet. "*Buenos noches, jefe.*"

"*Buenos noches, chica.*"

Chapter 9

To her later regret, Lilly declined the services of Hilario and instead decided to walk the eight blocks to her apartment. She felt light-headed, most likely due to the fact she hadn't eaten since the banana she had wolfed down in place of breakfast. Also, the cool night air aggravated her left leg. She had sustained a compound fracture of her femur some eight years before as a result of an auto accident. The accident occurred while driving a getaway car after an armored truck heist. It was how she ended up in prison. And it was in prison that a botched surgical repair left her with a permanent limp.

By the time she reached her apartment building, she was experiencing considerable discomfort. Once in the lobby, she punched in Kate's floor which was one floor above her own. She knew Kate would likely be home and studying if she wasn't watching mindless Mexican *telenovela* in an effort to improve her Spanish.

It had been a little more than year ago that Lilly and Jaime had been sent to Texas by Jeronimo to extract his newly found nineteen-year old granddaughter from a corrupt and dangerous life that she had fallen into by a combination of misjudgment, youth, and circumstance. Her misfortune had resulted in Kate and her then boyfriend becoming fugitives in four states, and charged as accessories in the shooting deaths of two Houston homicide detectives. It made little difference that she and her boyfriend had been no more than innocent bystanders.

Jeronimo had provided Kate refuge in Mexico City, much the same as what he had done for Lilly. Since then, the two women had grown close. Lilly became Kate's confidante, mentor, and a mother figure.

Kate was now a student at the university and seemed to be thriving in her new life; more than thriving to Lilly's amazement. It led Lilly to wonder if a feral life fraught with chaos and uncertainty might provide the perfect preparation for whatever life offered or threw at you. Lilly liked to think of herself as a graduate of that same school.

As she approached Kate's door she heard music coming from inside. From the beat, she guessed it to be the latest Cuban pop that was Kate's latest musical obsession. She hesitated for a moment before finally knocking. It wasn't until after the second knock that the door was flung open.

A skinny young man in a sleeveless white T-shirt and baggy jeans stood there with a beer bottle in one hand. His right ear was studded with what looked like at least eight earrings. He had a Van Gogh-style goatee and a mop of bushy dyed-blonde hair.

She guessed the guy's moronic grin was due to the marijuana, the skunky odor of which wafted through the open doorway like a fog bank. Lily tilted her head to look past him but didn't see Kate.

"*¿Quién eres?*" she asked without pretext.

They man's face slackened. He appeared to struggle to come up with a response. When he didn't, Lilly pushed past him.

"Espera!. ¿Qnuién eres?" he asked, the tone of his voice edged with bravado.

"Lilly. Is that you?" Kate shouted from somewhere in the back of the apartment. She emerged a few seconds later from her bedroom. She wore an open bathroom over a pair of shorts and a T-shirt.

"¿Qué pasa, tia?" she asked, her face beaming. "Did you meet Alex? We're taking French together. We were working on Parisian street lingo."

"I'll bet," Lilly said, not bothering to conceal her skepticism.

"This is Lilly" Kate said, turning to Alex. "I told you about her. Remember?"

"Mucho gusto," Alex said, offering up a nervous smile. "Mebbe I go," he said in halting English. He hurried over to the dining table and scooped up some books and what might have been a plastic baggie of pot. He stopped and gave Kate a peck on the cheek, muttered *mañana,* and scurried out the door.

"Did I scare him off?" Lilly asked.

Kate smiled. "Probably. One night when we were stoned I gave him a thumbnail sketch of what went down in Colorado."

"Do you think that was wise? What happened to impressing a boy with a French kiss? Did you show him the scar from your gunshot wound? Shit, you did. Didn't you?? Christ, Kate," she said when Kate offered a mischievous smile, "No wonder he took out of here so fast."

"Look, it's not what you think. We really were studying together."

"Okay, stick to that story. I just wanted to say goodbye and tell you to keep an eye on my plants. I have to sit. My leg is killing me," she said, wincing as she dropped into Kate's Barco lounger.

"Now where are you going? I mean, you must've just gotten back from Jalisco."

"I'm going to Texas. Austin. There's some business up there that Jaime needs help with."

"Who's Jaime? Didn't you use to date someone by that name?" she asked, feigning confusion. "I mean you guys seem to never see each other anymore."

There's some truth to that, Lilly thought. At times, she considered the possibility that Jeronimo purposefully kept them apart. He had never openly blessed their relationship, much less spoken of it other than in the context of a job, at least not until tonight.

"Yeah, well. Ships passing in the night. We're fine. Okay?" she added when Kate looked at her skeptically.

"It must be something serious if Jeronimo is sending both of you. The deadly duo to the rescue. Did you iron your cape and spray it with some of that bullet-proof shit? "

"You're stoned."

"Guilty. Believe it nor, but it helps with the French. I know. You don't have to warn me. But this is the only place I ever smoke. I never keep any *mota* here."

"If Jeronimo ever finds out, your ass is grass, no pun intended. Listen, the reason I stopped by…" She hesitated. "I was wondering if you still have one of those home pregnancy test kits lying around."

"Holy shit Lilly." Kate momentarily seemed to be a loss for words. "Maybe I should've been supplying you with condoms all this time."

"Stop it. You're not my mother."

Kate just grinned and shook her head.

"I've missed my periods before, I'm just making sure. Don't look at me like that. I'm still young enough to be… Just go check. Please."

Kate returned a minute later with two small boxes. "You'll let me know if I'm going to be an auntie."

"I'm probably not … pregnant." There she said it, although she still hadn't accepted the possibility, remote as it was. "I'll call you when I'm back," she said, hoping to change the subject.

"You know I'm on break. I've always wanted to go to Austin, I could…"

"Forget it, Kate. You know the States are off limits. Maybe one of these days you'll be able to go back to see your grandbabies."

"You be safe. Don't take any unnecessary chances. And stay close to Jaime. Okay?"

Stay close to Jaime. She could try, but that might prove difficult. She could only hope this would be over in a week's time. Something told her that would be unlikely. There would undoubtedly be fall out, for this was bound to be a messy venture.

She kissed Kate on both cheeks and went out the door.

Chapter 10
AUSTIN

Jaime pointed to his empty glass, signaling to the bartender to bring him a second tequila. They guy sitting in the stool next to Jaime raised his Heineken bottle to indicate he also needed another

The man was a hulking, sunburned construction contractor from Omaha with a burr haircut and more ink on his thick arms than the daily newspaper. He was here for the big construction convention, he mentioned to Jaime at least three times.

"Don't give my seat away," Jaime said, swiveling in his seat. "I gotta visit the head."

"Sure thing. It's yours unless she's pretty," the guy replied.

Jaime strolled casually in the wrong direction before abruptly reversing course, all the while allowing his eyes to survey the bar's occupants. It could be anybody, he decided. Earlier, he caught a young Hispanic-looking couple eyeing him from the end of the bar. They had left fifteen minutes earlier, giving up their seats to an elderly couple who looked too myopic to be a surveillance team.

He wasn't being paranoid. Someone was no doubt keeping tabs on him. Last evening, just before dusk, he `had walked the two blocks to the river, ostensibly to watch the hordes of bats swarm from beneath the Congress Avenue Bridge. He had spotted two possible tails, but lost sight of them amongst the large crowd of curious onlookers. That failed to dissuade him that he was being followed. The question was by whom? Becerra's people or the DEA? Or possibly both?

The Latina who had dropped him off at the hotel the previous morning had been overly circumspect about offering any information. Nothing about when he would be contacted much less by whom. All she had told him was that he was not to leave the hotel and keep his cell phone with him at all times. He ignored her orders and took a taxi back out to the airport to pick up a rental car. His only other transgression had been a stroll along the river. Otherwise, he had remained in his room watching NCIS reruns and subsisting on room service and the mini-bar.

This evening's foray to the hotel bar was the result of his boredom, but also by his desire to see if anyone would show their hand and approach him.

He had no sooner stepped up to a urinal when an Anglo guy in a cheap, rumpled suit walked in and made a show of washing his hands and his face. As dried his hands with a paper towel, he briefly made eye contact with Jaime who recognized the appraisal. Cop was written all over the guy, and it seemed a not so subtle attempt by the guy to confirm Jaime was indeed their subject.

Jaime waited at the urinal until the man left before washing up and making his way back to the bar. The conventioneer was gone, and in his place sat a woman with long red hair and wearing a strapless, shimmery black cocktail dress. He slid into his seat while giving her a sidelong glance.

She was attractive despite the excessively long fake eyelashes and her liver-colored lipstick. She didn't seem to pay him any mind as she scrolled through her cell phone.

His drink was still there, and he briefly entertained the possibility that the guy from Omaha had spiked his drink. Or maybe the would-be Mata Hari type sitting beside him had done it. Throwing caution to the wind, he took a long swallow.

The woman stuffed the cell phone into her purse and made a show of clicking her tongue in what seemed annoyance.

"I made sure they did not take your tequila," she said without turning to look at him.

He immediately recognized her voice, if not her appearance. It was the same Latina who had escorted him to the hotel the day before. Intrigued by this development, he studied her more closely as she turned to meet his gaze. If it wasn't for her voice, he would have never recognized her.

"Just tell me this," he said. "That young Hispanic couple sitting across from me earlier, were they your people?"

She merely looked at him.

"Besides the plainclothes cop in the restroom, who else is watching me?"

She offered him a slow, graceful shrug. *"No se.* I think mebbe many people watch us." She made a show of looking around the bar before turning back and smiling.

Her eyes were a dusty blue that didn't match her complexion. Surely contacts, he thought. She had thick black eyebrows that almost met in the middle. Her perfectly sculpted cheekbones were not likely the ones she had entered the world with. Her nose also looked almost too perfect. He had never thought of a nose as being erotic, but hers, both elegant and slightly upturned, made him want to reach up and slide his finger along the side of it.

"Last evening, you watched *los vampiros.* ¿Si? By the bridge," she said, taking a sip of her blue-colored cocktail. "I go there many times to watch them. It makes me think of home,"

"And where's that? Home?"

She pondered his question a moment before replying. "Monterrey. *En las monañas.* Near my home there was… *una caverna.* Every evening at nightfall, they would leave there to feed. The bats. I wanted to be like them," she added softly. "To be able to wander the night. *¿Eso tiene sentido?* What I mean by this?"

"Sure. You're telling me you're really a vampire. When do the fangs come out?"

She laughed, a brassy laugh that drew the attention of the customers sitting on the opposite side of the bar.

"*Pronto, tal vez.* Soon, yes? You must be careful. My bite is… *mortal.*"

"Great. Another biter," he muttered.

¿Qué?"

"So what's happening?" he asked, his patience wearing thin.

She studied him for a moment before replying. "I will tell you what it is you must do. You will become …*muy amoroso* with me. Yes? You will try to kiss me, and I will resist. *Tal vez,* I hit you. Slap you. No? *Pero* I leave. *Furioso.* You wait two minutes and go to *el baño.* There is a door that says Staff Only. Yes? Go through it and someone will meet you and bring you to me. ¿Lo *entiendes?"*

He took a swallow of his tequila, and without hesitating, he leaned his face into her neck. He caught a whiff of her perfume. Lavender, he thought as his lips grazed her ear. She immediately recoiled and shot him a look of disdain that seemed a bit overly dramatic. She almost stumbled in her haste to get off her stool before storming out past several tables of onlookers who stared at him. He offered them a sheepish grin and turned back to his drink.

He allowed his eyes to scan the bar to see if anyone had paid undue attention, but didn't see any obvious candidates. He downed his tequila and motioned for his tab.

The young Asian woman bartender placed two tabs in front of him. "The lady said you would buy her drink," she said with a barely concealed smirk.

He gave her three twenties and told her to keep the change. He gave it another minute, took one more look around the bar, and walked out. Sure enough, just past the restroom he found a door marked Staff Only. He hesitated and looked back, but the hallway remained empty.

The door opened to what appeared to be a laundry room. Leaning against a hamper was a young black man dressed in jeans and a white smock. He straightened and motioned for Jaime to follow him.

He led Jaime through the laundry room and into an adjacent storeroom that eventually opened onto a loading dock. The man turned, and without comment, strode back inside.

She stood leaning against the fender of a nondescript, late model compact. The red wig was gone and she had changed into jeans and a faded denim shirt. She blew a stream of smoke out of the side of her mouth and flicked the cigarette towards the dock.

"*Vamos. Apurarse!* Mebbe they follow you,' she said, opening the rear passenger side door he jumped off the dock and crawled in as she settled into the front passenger seat. The driver could've easily been the same guy who had greeted him curbside at the airport the day before.

Jaime had barely settled back into his seat before the driver accelerated into a U-turn and sped down a nearby alley onto the street in front of the hotel. He hung a quick left narrowly missing a couple of cars before cutting across a lane and swinging onto a broad, busy thoroughfare that Jaime recognized as Congress Avenue. The driver slipped the car seamlessly into the traffic before switching lanes, his eyes flicking back and forth in the rear view mirror.

The Latina turned and looked at him over the seat. "Now we go see *el jefe*," she said.

"I never caught your name."

"Soy Vera."

"Vera la Vampira," Jaime muttered beneath his breath.

"Teléfono," she said, turning to the driver who handed her a cell phone from his lap. She punched in a number and waited a moment before speaking. *"Nosotros estamos en camino,"* she said and handed the phone back to the driver. She looked at Jaime with an expression of mild curiously. "Now we shall see if you are useful as you say," she said, offering him a smile that managed to somehow look unpleasant.

Chapter 11

They drove several blocks down Congress Avenue in the direction of the looming, brightly illuminated edifice of the State Capitol. The driver made an abrupt right hand turn down a street that was clearly marked as one way in the opposite direction. He dodged a few cars blinking their lights and honking their horns before pulling into a parallel parking spot. Vera turned and stared out the rear window as the driver studied his rear view mirror.

"Seguir," she said, turning back forward.

The driver pulled out and took an immediate right turn onto a side street and then a left turn onto a street leading away from the downtown area. After several blocks they passed beneath a freeway and into a part of the city devoid of high rise buildings. Jaime caught the name on a street sign that indicated they were on East 12th Street.

The street appeared to be lined with bars, restaurants, and a variety of small commercial establishments; dry cleaners, liquor stores, a pharmacy. The murals painted on some of the walls suggested this was a section of the city where the population was more heavily black and Hispanic. The few houses evident appeared older and gentrified.

They drove for perhaps ten or so minutes before turning into an alleyway beside what looked to be a small bar sporting a neon sign that said simply "Lucky Fredo". A dark-colored, older model Econoline van along with a couple of pickup trucks and a 60's era low rider convertible appeared to be the only vehicles in the small parking lot in the rear of the bar. The driver pulled in next to the Ford van and cut the ignition.

"Come, Jaime" Vera said, dismounting.

The driver also got out and proceeded to pat Jaime down, checking for weapons or a wire. He retrieved the cell phone from Jaime's trouser pocket and put it in his own pocket before nodding his approval to Vera.

The thought crossed Jaime's mind that if he was indeed about to meet with Miguel Becerra how simple it might be to alert the police of the location of a wanted fugitive. Game set match. It would be over. That is if he still had his cell phone. Prudence suggested he should first wait and see what transpired.

Vera led Jaime across the deeply rutted parking lot and through a grated screen door that opened into a store room stacked to the ceiling with cases of beer and cardboard boxes containing sundry food stuffs, mostly chips and *chicharones* from what he could see. The room reeked of stale beer and the unmistakable aroma of marijuana. From the direction of the bar he caught a mariachi riff and a familiar song – the Mexican pop star Paulina Rubio singing *El Ultimo Adios*.

He followed Vera through a beaded curtain into a room not much larger than the average living room. To the right was a crude bar flanked with neon signs advertizing Pacifico and Corona beer.

Sitting at a table to Jaime's left were three slack-jawed men in sleeveless T-shirts. They turned in unison to study Jaime like a trio of hungry wolves in sunglasses. In the corner next to them, a pair of young girls slouched like a couple of forgotten parcels.

Vera took Jaime's arm and pulled him towards a booth in the far corner occupied by two men. The one sitting with his back to the corner was a handsome, olive complexioned man of perhaps forty dressed in a black T-shirt and a silvery sport coat. His stylishly-coifed head of black hair glistened in the piss-yellow light from the low-hanging florescent light hanging above the booth.

He gave Jaime a look of open appraisal before nodding to his equally well-attired companion who immediately slid from the booth and walked off, but not before Jaime noted the large handgun protruding from the man's waistband.

Vera indicated to Jaime that he should take a seat in the vacated bench. She slid in beside him.

The man that Jaime assumed was Miguel Becerra had a handsome, round face, a two day old growth of beard, and pale, deep-set eyes that imparted a watery brightness.

He stared at Jaime for a long moment before uncoupling his eyes to gaze across the room. When he turned back, his eyes displayed the kind of cold menace one practiced in front of a mirror.

"We will speak English. There are too many ears," he said in heavily-accented English. "Vera says they are watching you.

La chota . Tal vez La DEA." He looked at Vera. "You are clean? *Si.*"

"No one followed us."

"I imagine if they knew you were here in the States they'd be all over you by now," Jaime said.

Becerra didn't reply.

"Look, enough of the cat and mouse crap. Let's talk business," Jaime said.

"The cat and the mouse," Becerra said, smiling. "I like that. Like in the cartoons, Tom and Jerry, yes? I watched them when I was a child. *Muy bien.* What is it you wish?"

"Hold on. Your guy approached me. Remember? What do you want?"

Becerra nodded an inch. "Betrayal is… *complicado.* To betray someone, that does not …" He shrugged. "How can I say? It makes it difficult to place one's trust in someone willing to betray their boss. I must ask you why you do this, for money. Or is it … *tal vez resentimiento?* Resentment I believe is the word in English, Yes?"

"How about if I told you I was there the night Jeronimo killed your brother?"

He stared at Jaime, his face betraying nothing. The last chorus of *El Ultimo Adios* faded away, the ensuing silence filled by the buzzing of the florescent light above their heads.

"I drove up and saw your brother kneeling in the dirt, his hands behind his head. Hermosa was standing behind him, and…"

"*¡Deja de hablar! Suficiente.*" Becerra glared at him. "Why do you tell me this?" he said, seeming to struggle to regain his composure.

"I tell you this because Hermosa is a man without honor. He killed your brother who he said was like a son to him. It seems it is easy for him to discard loyalty."

Becerra reached for a cigarette from the pack at his elbow. He lighted his cigarette, lifting his chin to blow a stream of smoke towards the ceiling, all the while his eyes fixed on Jaime.

"There is a woman," Jaime went on. "She finds herself employed by a man who places her in his trust. She feels very fortunate to be in such a position. She believes that she is protected by this man."

"Hermosa?"

Jaime nodded. "But he begins to have doubts about the woman. *La paranoia.* He no longer trusts her. He feels she knows too many things about his business. He decides he must rid himself of her."

Becerra shook his head in what might have been empathy. Jaime waited a moment before going on.

"This woman is someone I care about. I won't allow Hermosa to harm her."

"So you betray him out of your feelings for this woman? Is that what you wish for me to believe?" he said with a smile.

"First, he gets rid of this woman. And then? Who's to say I won't be next. He is that kind of a man."

Becerra said nothing.

"This woman…" Vera began to interject but Becerra held up his hand to silence her, his eyes fixed steadily on Jaime as if measuring his veracity.

"Women are… What is the expression you Americans like to use? A dime a dozen. Yes?" He glanced at Vera and smiled. ¿No *es cierto, chica?*"

Vera said nothing.

Becerra took a long pull on his cigarette and gazed across the room at the three *chulos* sitting at the table. "I trust no one, *Señor Soledad.* I ask again. What is it you propose?"

Jaime hesitated, shifting nervously in his seat and looking around the room. He hoped his body language might convey to Becerra that he was rightfully nervous. That he was taking a great risk.

"You wish Hermosa dead. So do I. Okay?"

Becerra said nothing.

"I told Hermosa that this business with his hotel required his personal attention. The hotel manager has refused to deal with me, but instead wishes to negotiate directly with my boss. I'm guessing that was at your instruction. It was difficult convincing Hermosa, but in the end, he agreed. As a matter of fact, he is arriving here tomorrow. Now, tell me what is it that you propose?"

Becerra appeared to digest what Jaime had told him for a long moment before replying. "First, you must tell me what is it you wish in return?"

"The life of the woman I love for one thing."

Now the hook, Jaime thought, his gaze circling the room before looking back at Becerra.

"I also need your help in taking over Hermosa's Mexico City operation. You have to understand that I'm not a greedy man. You would get your share of course. It could prove rewarding for the both of us."

"*Posiblimente*. You must know that we are facing opposition… *compentencia* from our brothers in Sinaloa. For now at least, we hold the upper hand n Mexico City. Your boss has refused to deal with us or the Sinaloa. It would be good if Hermosa was no longer interfering with our business in *la ciudad*."

"Then we have a deal?"

"I wish to consider this more carefully. Discuss it with others."

"Fair enough. I'll wait to hear from you."

"I do not need to tell you that you will be watched. Not only by us. If there is any indication you are… playing with me, I will deal with you myself. *¿Entiendes?*"

Jaime nodded. Becerra looked at Vera. "Return him to his hotel," he said with a dismissive wave of his hand.

Vera took Jaime's arm and gestured with her head to indicate the audition was over. As they walked out, one of the *chulos* sitting at the table appeared to sneer at him. Jaime shot him the finger.

"Can I trust him?" Jaime asked once they were back out in the parking lot.

"This is a dangerous game we play, yes? But we play anyway. *La confianzo es un bien barato.* It is cheap. This trust we must give. Does that answer your question? Now let us go back to your room and finish our drinks. You can tell me about your woman."

Chapter 12

He hoped that by allowing Vera to accompany him to his room it might prove productive if there might be any chance that she might enlighten him regarding Becerra or his intentions. He assumed that Vera had no doubt been tasked by Becerra to do pretty much the same. It would be a balancing act. His instincts and past experience ferreting out duplicity told him to approach Vera with caution. She might prove to be another wild card in a game that at this point he felt he had no other choice but to allow to play out.

The driver dropped them off at the same loading dock in the rear of the hotel where they were met by the same young black man as before. He escorted them past a group of black women sorting laundry to a service elevator before withdrawing with a simple nod of his head.

Vera retrieved what appeared to be a pass card from her pocket and inserted it into a slot beside the bank of floor buttons. She punched in one of the high floors.

"We will not go to your room, she said, leaning back against the elevator wall. "We go to a special room In case they bug your room."

"They being who?"

"*Policia, La DEA.* It is not like they do not know about us. Or watch us." She offered him a shrug of acceptance. "It is the way it must be. Here we live in *las sombras.* It is different than in Mexico. Yes?"

He didn't reply, his thoughts focused on the unsettling prospect of a special room. He wondered at the likelihood that his room really might be bugged. If he was already on someone's radar, then there was the chance all of this had already been compromised. And if so, then Vera might not be the only wild card.

He took the opportunity to study her more closely. In the stark glare of the elevator's overhead light, she looked older despite her smooth, unlined face. Perhaps, it was just her eyes which betrayed what he took to be a measure of melancholia and fatigue. Her tight-fitting jeans revealed her wide hips and slim waist.

The elevator opened on the eighth floor, and Vera led him to a room at the very end of hallway. It was a large suite that offered a view across the river. The room seemed to have been unoccupied for quite some time for it smelled stuffy, and unlike every other hotel room in Texas, it wasn't as frigid as a meat locker. The bed was neatly made and the glasses on the dresser were still wrapped in cellophane.

Vera adjusted the thermostat before closing the drapes. "No bugs here," she declared, turning on a bedside lamp. A bottle of what appeared to be tequila sat on the night stand. She twisted off the seal and handed it to him.

"*Perdoneme,*" she said and disappeared into the bathroom.

He poured them each a drink and took a seat. A moment later, he heard the toilet flush and she emerged, her cell phone in her hand. She was like a chameleon, for something in her body language told him that she had reverted back to the role of the seductress she had played earlier in the bar downstairs. She plucked her drink from the dresser and settled into one of the other chairs.

"You know Miguel does not trust you. Or believe what you say," she said, downing half her drink.

"Well, the feeling is mutual. *Mutuo.* You never really said if you trust him."

She looked at him in a way that suggested she was carefully considering her answer.

"You say Hermosa does not trust your woman. Miguel is no different."

"Meaning he doesn't trust you?"

She didn't replay at first, "There are things you should know before you place your fortunes in Miguel's hands." She paused to top off her glass from the bottle on the nightstand.

"My father had a dog. *Un pero guardian.* To watch over his car, he would say. It was a good dog for such a thing. But you learned never to turn your back on such a dog."

"You're saying Miguel is like that dog?"

She shrugged. "*Tal vez.*"

"How long have you known him?"

She stared at him over her glass as she took a long swallow. "Since we were children. Often we play together. Miguel and me. His father was a *vaquero* on my father's *finca*."

"What is it exactly that you do for him?"

"Probably I do much like you do for Hermosa. I take care of certain problems. I watch and listen."

"And he wants you to watch me. To listen to what I tell you?"

She gave a slight nod. "Miguel believes you can be useful. Or wishes it so."

"He wants me to kill my boss."

"No, he wishes to do that. You must only deliver him." She took a swallow of her tequila before going on. "You should know that no matter what you wish to believe, Miguel will become your boss. And then neither of you can turn your back on the other. Yes?" she said with a smile.

He nodded in agreement.

She finished her drink and set her glass on the night stand.

Chapter 13

"I will tell you a story," she said after a long moment had passed. "One day, Miguel and his brother Ramon steal one of my father's saddles. It was a very expensive saddle with *micha plata*. Silver. My father's favorite."

"Ramon was Miguel's brother? The one Hermosa killed."

"*Si*. My father, he discovers that they steal from him. He makes their father whip them. Very badly. The next day Miguel and Ramon run away."

"Many years go by and then one day Miguel comes to my father's *hacienda*. He kills my father with a machete. I saw this," she added, pulling her eyes away.

She stared at the empty glass on the nightstand and looked back at him. "I did not care so much that Miguel killed my father. My father was not a good man. He was a cruel father. After Miguel does this, he takes me," she said, her voice flat and free of emotion. "¿Lo *entiendes*? What I mean by this?"

"I take it that he wasn't rescuing you."

She hesitated before answering. "He has kept me by his side for many years."

"Against your will? Or as his lover?"

Her whole body seemed to stiffen. "¿Su *amanate?* I am not sure you can call it that. Lovers? *Si, pero sin afecto.*"

"But you are... What to him? I mean what's the connection?"

"You wish to know how it is that I am with this man. Why I work for him."

He looked at her but said nothing. Another long moment passed during which she seemed to slip away in thought. Finally, she sighed deeply as if to clear her mind. She leaned forward in her chair and looked past him as if gazing at some distant horizon.

"There was a time when Miguel was not cruel. Before he became involved with the cartels, he was... *diferente.* You wish to know if I loved him. There was a time when I had feelings for him. *No más. ¿Lo entiendes?*"

He nodded. This was the last direction Jaime expected this conversation to go but he remained silent. It was obvious there was more to this story, and far be it from him to interrupt.

"I tell you these things, *pero...* Do not misunderstand. I do not choose to tell you these things because I trust you. Because I do not. I trust no one. I tell you things to... What is the word? To rid myself of things. Unburden, I believe is the word. To unburden my soul."

"And why would you do that?"

"*No sé. Tal vez, estoy cansada.* And telling this to a stranger is sometimes more easy."

He was beginning to think the waters were growing murkier by the minute.

"I still don't understand why you stay. You can't leave him?"

She shook her head. "Because… *Es muy complicado.* Many times I do not understand the things that I do."

"Rear view mirrors are always twenty twenty," he muttered. "And he still trusts you?"

"It is much like with your woman and Hermosa. Miguel trusts no one. No, I believe he no longer trusts me," she added, staring at him intently. "Why I stay…."

She reached for the bottle of tequila and splashed a generous amount into her glass.

"*Quedé embarazada,*" she said so softly that he had to lean closer in order to hear her. "With his child." She took a swallow of her tequila before going on.

"I am allowed to see my daughter one time each year. On her birthday. Alma is her name. She is ten. This is cruel? No? Miguel says he keeps her away from me so she will be safe. Away from this," She gestured vaguely over her shoulder. She took another swallow of her tequila.

"And to keep me," she added. "And yes. I try to find her. To take her away. *Pero…*It is not so simple."

Here comes the pitch, he thought. Does he bite or wait her out? Nibble, not bite, he decided, pouring himself another drink.

"And if you find your daughter and if Miguel was… out of the way."

He wanted to ask if she really thought she could pull something like that off and get away with it.

"It is the only way."

"What are you saying, Vera?"

"That we can both be free from our bosses. ¿No *esta claro?*"

He didn't reply, allowing the silence to buy him time. Jeronimo's plan was to rid himself of Becerra, just not in the way Vera might be proposing. She obviously preferred Becerra dead. And she thought Jaime wanted the same fate for Jeronimo. At this point, he wasn't sure if her proposal might prove to an advantage or an unnecessary complication.

"You need to give this some serious thought," he said finally. "This thing you want to do. *Es muy peligroso.*"

"*Pero es una oportunidad. ¿*Si? You do not agree?"

"Like I said, you need to think about it "

"Does that mean you would not consider this?"

"I meant we both need to think about it.

She placed her empty glass on the night stand. "I must go"

"And report to Miguel?"

"*Si.* "

"What will you say?

"That you have great hatred for Jeronimo Hermosa. And that you are greedy. He will like that. That you are greedy. *Un hermano.*"

"Where is he now? Where does he stay when he's here?"

She looked at him quizzically. "I never know such things He is….*muy sospechosos. Paranocio.* He stays at a different house every night. He calls me when he needs something." She eyed him with what seemed renewed curiosity. "We have not talked about your woman," she said, pushing to her feet. "*Tal vez,* another time."

She threw open the curtains, adjusted the thermostat, and walked out without saying another word.

He sat there thinking. This could easily be a trap on Becerra's part – a way of testing him. Vera's story sounded too much like something from a Mexican *telenovela.* There was no way to check the veracity of her story. He would just have to believe it or not. It would be interesting to hear what Jeronimo thought of this latest wrinkle. He finished his drink and walked out.

Chapter 14

Vera took the elevator to the lobby instead of going to her room. She knew Miguel would be waiting for her and wanting to know what she had found out. As she expected, a black SUV was parked across the street. She shook her head. Miguel was being naïve; if not dangerously foolhardy, to believe no one was watching. His ego knew no bounds, nor his stupidity. She was amazed he had survived the treacherous internal conniving the cartels were known for. It worried her for he was putting her life on the line as well as his own. She waited for the traffic to clear and hurried across the street and crawled into the back seat.

He made no obvious acknowledgement of her appearance, but instead continued puffing on his cigarette.

"Tenías razón. El…"

He held up his hand to stop her. "English, please," Becerra said.

She knew of his habit of selecting drivers who spoke little to no English. It was another sign of his naiveté to think his drivers didn't possess the basic rudiments of English. Did he really think his drivers didn't surf the internet or watch movies?

"You were right about him," she said, starting over. "He is greedy and foolish." Just like you she wanted to say.

"So you still believe he will deliver Hermosa to me?"

"I have no doubt. It is simply a matter of time. He says we must wait until it can be easily done."

Becerra shook his head. "I have no time to wait. There are matters back home I must attend to."

She knew the real crux of the matter was that he could not risk being away from the centers of power in the cartel for too long and thus give his enemies time to scheme.

"So what is it you wish me to do?"

"You followed him back to the airport, yes?"

"*Si.* He rented a car."

He reached into his pocket and retrieved a small object the size of a cigarette pack. She recognized it immediately. It was a transponder, a tracking device. She had used one before on two other occasions.

"You will attach this to his rental. It is important we know his whereabouts at all times. Understood?"

She took it from and dropped it into her purse. "You want me to follow him?"

"*Si.* Hermosa will stay at his hotel. I must know how many people he travels with. How many bodyguards. He is not stupid. He will expect that he is being watched. I must know about those who watch him. And also who remains in the shadows. You understand what I say?"

"Perfectamente. How do I reach you?'

He reached into his pocket again and pulled out what she knew was a burner phone.

"You must only call if it is important. Now go."

She got out and watched as the SUV drove off. She only wished she could place some kind of tracking device on his car. It would make it all so much simpler. She slipped the transponder into her purse and walked back across the street.

Chapter 15

Their flight to Austin left late due to a violent thunderstorm. As a result, they spent almost an hour on the tarmac waiting out the storm. Fortunately, Lilly's business class seat was quite comfortable. From where she sat, she caught occasional glimpses of Jeronimo and Ernesto in the First Class cabin.

Jeronimo had been adamant that Lilly remain on the sidelines and out of sight. Therefore, she had gone out of her way to keep her distance at the airport in case Jeronimo might be under observation.

She had even gone so far as to don a black wig and tie it back in a severe bun. Her contacts had been replaced with heavy-framed reading glasses. She wore a mid-calf length black skirt, a rather shopworn gray sweater, and a pair of clunky shoes a friend referred to as the kind usually worn by stealth nuns.

She looked nothing like the photos on either of her two false passports. For this trip, she carried a passport proclaiming she was Lilia Zamorra and had never before traveled to the US.

The year before when entering the US, she had used her other false passport, the one bearing the name Lilia Montez. She worried that if she used that passport the computers at Immigration might show she had arrived in Houston, but there would be no record of her exiting the US. There was no sense taking a risk.

In addition, secreted into the lining of her purse was a California driver's license issued to Layla Carter along with a VISA credit card linked to one of Jeronimo's shell companies.

Also folded amongst her panties and a box of tampons was the home pregnancy test kit Kate had given her. She wasn't entirely sure why she hadn't taken the test that morning before leaving for the airport. Part of her kept assuring herself that she would start her period any day now. And part of her remained in simple denial as to the possibility the test would be positive. She didn't want to think about it. She couldn't think about it. Not under the current circumstances. Denial and procrastination seemed the better options.

Once they were airborne, she took out her laptop and began researching Austin. She flipped through dozens of images of the city, as well as the pages meant for first time visitors. She had no need to read about the trendy restaurants, the best place for Tex-Mex, the museums, the many night clubs, or the shopping malls. She was searching instead for the city's underbelly.

She found a site that detailed the history of the Austin drug culture from the heyday of marijuana smuggling in the 70, to cocaine in the 80's, and to the present day where there was a smorgasbord of just about every illicit substance known to man. The millions of tourists, the large student population, the relatively affluent young age demographic, its reputation as a music and party town, and finally its proximity to Mexico all served to ensure a drug culture to flourish.

Jeronimo had been right in his account of how all this, in addition to the city's size, diversity, and infrastructure made it an appealing location for the cartels to secure a presence.

Consequently, there also existed plenty of law enforcement surveillance from the local and state narcotics units as well as the DEA. There was even a Justice Department task force comprised of all these actors.

She wondered what the chances were that any of these agencies might be aware of Jeronimo's impending arrival. She assumed Jeronimo would also be traveling on a false passport. Jeronimo had assured her that there were no warrants for his arrest in the States. Whether he was even a person of interest was doubtful. But if they did detect his arrival, it would surely make this game even more of a gamble and more dangerous.

She glanced up and saw Ernesto strolling down the aisle in her direction. He made brief eye contact with her as he passed by, but otherwise gave no indication of recognition. A moment later, he dropped his heavy bulk in the empty seat next to her.

"No hay nadie," he said, wheezing from even the mild exertion of walking the aisles.

It made her wonder again if Ernesto was the right choice for this kind of job.

"¿Estas seguro?" she asked, looking up from her laptop.

"Si. No one." He looked at her and smiled. "I have a… way with such things. *Mi radar.*"

She realized that months had likely passed since the two of them had exchanged more than the usual pleasantries. Their paths rarely crossed due to their division of labor. Ernesto worked in the trenches so to speak, collecting protection money and debts, and ensuring that Jeronimo's edicts were being followed. From what she had learned, he had been with Jeronimo since the beginning, first serving as a gofer, then a body guard, and later as his strong arm. His loyalty to *el jefe* was without question.

It appeared obvious that in his younger days he must have possessed an imposing physique. Even now, his stout girth no doubt concealed a bed rock of muscle. His fleshy face also belied what was once a handsome visage. His only blemish was a smooth, purplish worm of a scar that ran the length of his right jawbone. The word on the street was the scar was the result of an adversary's failed attempt to cut Ernesto's throat. Various stories also speculated on the adversary's fate, none of which had happy endings for his assailant.

He possessed an easy smile that could easily morph into a glower of menace. Jeronimo was probably right in saying Ernesto was not someone to underestimate.

"How's your English, Ernesto?" she asked, closing her laptop.

He gave an equivocal shake of his head and took a deep breath. "*Mi esposa…* My wife, she likes to come to the… outlet malls. Is that not what they are called? So, I go with her one, two times every year. There is a very large such mall near Austin. She shops. I watch people and listen to what they say. I watch American television. The police shows. I like the Law and Order, but I don't understand the trial parts so much. American *sistema de justica. Complicado.*"

"You'll get no argument there."

Ernesto nodded and smiled in such a way that indicated her comment had gone past him.

"Dime, Ernesto. Es Jeronimo…"

He held up his hand. "Please, Lilia. *En ingles, por favor.* I must begin to think in English."

"Okay. Tell me. You are his friend. Is this wise? This thing he wishes to do?"

Ernesto opened his mouth as if to reply, then hesitated. "Yes, I am his friend," he said with a nod. "Since we were young men. But he is also my boss. I must always do as he asks. Without question. This thing he wishes to do. Yes I have many questions. I believe concerns is the correct word. Even if this is done correctly, I fear there will be…" He laughed. "There is a new word I learn watching the Law and Order. Blowback. Yes? From Jalisco."

"And I told him that also."

"He is *obstinado*. And sometimes reckless. But this…" He shrugged. "It has become *personal*. This thing between them. He and Becerra." When she didn't reply, he went on. "We must trust Jaime He is a good man, *Capaz*. Capable, you agree?"

Capable and overly confident she wanted to say. "We'll see. We play it by ear. ¿Si?"

"Tocar de oido. Yes. Now I must go back or he will worry," he said, pushing to his feet with considerable effort.

She watched him shamble slowly back up the aisle. We better hope there aren't any foot races, she thought. She just hoped that she would be able to stay close enough to handle any situation that arose. It couldn't just be Jaime and Jeronimo who were in harm's way. She would make sure of that.

Chapter 16
AUSTIN

Jeronimo had booked Lilly a room at *La Casa de los Colibries,* his troubled boutique hotel, under her California *nom de guerre,* He and Ernesto planned to stay in the private bungalow on the rear of the property.

After picking up her rental car at the airport, Lilly took her time making her way to the hotel, taking a detour that took her down First Street and skirted the edges of the Travis Heights neighborhood where the hotel was located. Besides wanting to check out the lay of the land and check for tails, she also wanted to also ensure she wouldn't arrive at the same time as Jeronimo and Ernesto.

After checking in, she jettisoned the wig and the glasses and exchanged the drab clothes for a pair of jeans and a University of Texas sweatshirt she purchased at the airport. She also bought a snappy brown leather beret. Within an hour of her settling into her room, Jeronimo texted her that Jaime had contacted him and was expected at the hotel later that afternoon. She knew without asking that she was now tasked with seeing who might be observing the hotel.

Casa de los Colibries was situated in Travis Heights, an older residential section of South Austin that was separated from the gleaming towers of downtown Austin by Lady Bird Lake, formerly known as the Town Lake, and before that, the Colorado River. The neighborhood had been founded in the 1920's as an upscale development and had gone though several previous iterations.

Now it consisted of a mix of older, tastefully refurbished houses, more modest-sized gentrified homes, small apartment complexes and pocket parks that lined a meandering limestone creek bed. It was a highly sought after part of town where even modest fixer-uppers fetched upwards of a million dollars in resale value.

Jeronimo had bought the acreage now occupied by this hotel from an elderly matron in Mexico City who had inherited it from her father, a prominent international attorney who had the house built as a wedding gift for his wife in 1930. When the couple died in a plane crash, it passed into the hands of their only child, a daughter who had married a Mexican film actor.

The daughter had no intention of returning to Texas, and so the house subsequently fell into neglect and disrepair. Over the years, numerous developers had attempted to wrest it from the old lady's grip, but their offers always fell on deaf ears. Her hesitation to sell the property had more to do with her obstinate eccentricity than any affinity she held for the house. It was only in her last year of life that Jeronimo was able to use his social connections and a fair amount of persuasion to get her to part with the now derelict property.

The house, built in the style of a Southern plantation mansion, had been surrounded by three acres of fallow land overgrown with poison oak and waist-high Johnson grass. A pair of large live oak shaded what remained of a semi-circular drive. A forlorn stand of half-dozen or so pecan trees graced the rear of the property.

It required eighteen months and a considerable amount of investment for Jeronimo to restore the house and grounds to their former glory. Now it was a nine hundred dollar a night boutique hotel that featured carefully manicured grounds that included a conservatory and an aviary, a pool, a spa, and even a small indoor movie theater.

Within three months of its opening, the problems began. First, there was a ruptured water main that seemed suspiciously to be the result of vandalism. Then a handful of the staff abruptly quit, followed by a spate of food poisoning among the guests. A month ago, the first manager disappeared under cover of night. Soon after, Jaime had been sent to sort it out and right the ship.

His initial investigation left little doubt that someone was doing their best to ensure the hotel would fail. He managed to locate several of the former staff who initially refused to talk to him. He finally persuaded one of them to admit to being physically threatened if he remained. The former manager had fled to Costa Rica and couldn't be found.

It was only when Jaime bribed a former security guard that he was able to follow the trail to the doorstep of a Mexican attorney and fixer with ties to the Jalisco cartel.

Somehow, his inquiries had come to the attention of a certain Miguel Becerra. One night while Jaime was walking to his car outside of a restaurant, he was intercepted by two men who left him little choice but to accompany them to a waiting Cadillac Escalade where one of Becerra's minions waited.

Hence, an initial proposal was floated. Jaime saw it as more like one of those offers one couldn't refuse. It was either a watery grave in the bottom of Lady Bird Lake or the prospect of betraying his boss.

All of this was recounted to Lilly by Jeronimo the evening before their departure from Mexico City. Jeronimo, perhaps purposefully, had been somewhat vague about any details regarding Jaime's exact role in this subterfuge other than his bogus betrayal. It made her wonder if there actually was really any sort of concrete plan or they would all be winging it. There seemed to be too many moving parts. Locating Becerra would be one thing. Getting DEA or local law enforcement to make a move was something all together different.

After unpacking her bag, Lilly slung her small backpack over her shoulder and strode to the end of the hotel's drive to survey the street in both directions. To her left, halfway down the block was what appeared to be a small park. A small group of people, most of them children, appeared to be having a picnic. The two cars parked nearby appeared to be empty. She decided one of the benches next to the sidewalk would provide a good vantage spot to watch the comings and goings on at the hotel. To her right, four houses down, a Penske rental van sat parked in the drive of one of the houses.

She began walking down the street in the van's direction but on the opposite side of the street. As she drew near, she saw someone sitting in the driver's seat. At the end of the block, she stood and pretended to look in both directions before walking back towards the Penske van, this time on the other side of the street.

She approached the back of the van and circled around to the driver's side. She startled the man in the driver's seat with her unexpected appearance to the point that he spilled the contents of a Styrofoam cup in his lap. She heard him curse as she began rapping on his window. He stared at her for a few seconds before rolling the window down halfway.

"Can I help you?" he asked brusquely

"I'm sorry, but I was told there was a grocery right around the corner, but I don't see it. Do you know far away it is?" she asked with a smile.

Her eyes, concealed behind her mirrored sunglasses, took a quick inventory of the dash and empty passenger seat. On the seat, a newspaper partially concealed what appeared to be a camera with a telescopic lens. Two cell phones sat on the dash.

"I'm sorry; ma'am, but we're movers and I really don't know this part of town," he said dismissively and began rolling up the window.

"How about a bus stop? Have you seen one?"

Out of the corner of her eye, she thought she saw movement in the back of the van.

"I'm sorry," he said with obvious irritation and rolled up the window.

Lilly nodded, turned and walked back in the direction of the hotel. A surveillance team for sure, she thought. But whose? Whoever they were, they had most likely followed Jeronimo and Ernesto from the airport. It made her wonder about Jeronimo's assurance that he wasn't the likely target of any surveillance. If so, who were the people in the van?

She casually strolled down to the park and claimed a bench that offered an unrestricted view of the hotel. Taking out her paperback and thermos of coffee from her backpack, she settled in for the wait.

Chapter 17

The traffic on the street in front of the hotel was relatively light. An occasional pedestrian strolled by the hotel and disappeared around the corner.

None of the pedestrians appeared to be loitering unnecessarily with the exception of a woman in a shapeless, gray-colored smock and a baseball cap pushing a baby stroller. When the woman reached the corner, she paused to talk on her cell phone for a few minutes before turning back in the direction of the hotel. As she approached the driveway, she stopped again to retrieve her cell phone from her bag.

It was then that a small SUV pulled into the hotel's drive and parked in front of the hotel. Even from this distance, she recognized Jaime as he dismounted. He wore jeans, a white dress shirt and carried a briefcase. He paused to look around before disappearing behind the shrubs in front of the hotel.

The woman in the smock put away her phone and began walking back in Lilly's direction, but on the opposite side of the street. As she drew abreast of Lilly, she gave Lilly a quick glance although it was difficult to tell if she actually was looking at

Lilly due to the woman's over-sized sunglasses and the baseball cap pulled low over her long blonde hair. The woman leaned over the stroller and appeared to say something to her child before continuing on down the sidewalk.

Lilly watched the woman for a moment. Something about seeing the woman pushing a stroller elicited a pang of anxiety. She still hadn't done the pregnancy test, partially because her nausea had abated, and also because she had convinced herself that she really wasn't that late starting her period.

She had never been one to yearn for motherhood. The occasional fantasy about that possibility had been cut short by the realities of her life. She had thought she had become pregnant with Harlan that time in Idaho, but it proved to be a false alarm. She had suffered a miscarriage with Estevan. All for the best, she thought. She conceded that she simply wasn't mother material.

She put these thoughts aside and returned to her paperback, occasionally looking up to see if the street provided any new action. A half-hour passed without activity before she noticed a tall, somewhat heavy-set black man sauntering casually toward her from the direction of the hotel. She gave him only slight attention until he drew near to her bench. He stopped, turned and looked back in the direction of the hotel, and then without a moment of hesitation, came and sat on the bench beside her.

He wore khakis, a pink polo shirt, and a pair of Reeboks. He had the bulky, fleshy builds of a professional football player gone to seed. Gauging from his gray, closely-cropped hair and the fine delta of wrinkles at the corner of his eyes, Lilly guessed his age at somewhere between forty and fifty. He held the stub of a half-smoked cigar in his one hand.

After sitting, he seemed to cast an empty stare at the line of shrubs across the street. She studied him out of the corner of her eyes for a moment before closing her paperback. He turned and looked at her.

"I'm sorry. Am I interrupting your reading?" He had a deep, baritone voice and a distinctly Southern accent.

"No, not at all. I just finished a chapter."

"What are you reading if you don't mind me asking?"

"Elmore Leonard. Out of Sight."

"Oh, that was a good one. Did you ever see the movie with Clooney and JLo?"

She remembered seeing it in the prison at Perryville. It had fueled her fantasies of breaking out, and sure enough six months later she had been smuggled out of the prison in a laundry hamper. It was all part of a scheme by the Feds to enlist her help in locating a gunrunner who happened to be her former bank robber accomplice. It had almost gotten her killed, but at least she had escaped another ten years of incarceration. Another story and another life, she thought.

"Nope, never did. Are you a fan of his? Leonard, I mean."

"You could say so. I even got the opportunity to play poker with him once. Lost my ass, too." He studied her intently in a way that for some reason made her uncomfortable. "Do you live around here?" he asked, retrieving a lighter from his pocket and relighting the stub of cigar.

"No. I'm just visiting," she replied.

Somehow this wasn't beginning to sound like small talk.

He nodded and looked at her. "That little charade back at the van was actually pretty good. Tell me, did you ever used to be on the job?"

"I'm not sure what you mean?"

"Come on. Tell me who it is that you're keeping an eye out for? Mr. Soledad, maybe. Or someone else?"

She stared at him as she fumbled for a reply.

"Listen, I think you've made a mistake, I wasn't watching for anyone. I'm just sitting here minding my own business. Unlike you," she said, trying her best to rein in her anger.

"Come now, Miss Carter. If that's really your name. Who are you working for? I don't take you for some cartel flunky. Unless maybe you're a freelancer. I already checked to see if you're somebody from the task force that they didn't bother to tell us about. That leaves Hermosa.

He took a puff of his cigar before going on. "I reached out to an acquaintance in Mexico City who keeps tabs on organized crime there. It seems Hermosa has a girl Friday. An American by the name of Lilia Montez. Or is it Lilia Zamora? I'd give anything to know what your real name is. If you give me enough time, I'll bet I can find out."

"What do you want?" There seemed to be no longer any reason to remain coy.

"I told you. I'm curious who you're expecting to see. I'm guessing it's any cartel types creeping around."

She smiled. "I could ask you the same thing. Who might you be watching for?"

He looked at her for a long moment before replying. "We're not sure yet what kind of game you people are running here. I'll just say we don't take kindly to the cartels holding their business meetings on our turf. Tell that to your boss," he said, getting to his feet. "And maybe you should warn Soledad that the woman he's consorting with is a hitter for Jalisco. My guess is she's here to take out your boss. He'd best be careful." He nodded goodbye and walked off in the direction of the Penske van.

"Fuck," she muttered. So much for staying in the shadows, she thought. If the Feds had picked up on her, who else might be on to her? If the Feds were watching Jeronimo it meant they knew something. They obviously knew about Jaime. And what did the Fed mean when he said Jaime was consorting with a woman from the Jalisco cartel? A hitter at that. By hitter, she assumed he meant a hit man. A hit woman in this case.

"Dammit!" It suddenly occurred to her that if they knew what name she was registered under at the hotel then they also knew her room number. If so, they could easily lift her finger prints from the door handle or her luggage. It would just be a matter of time before they caught on to her real identity. She wondered if it was already too late to wipe her prints from everything in the room she had touched.

She also assumed they would flag her passport. It would make it difficult to get back to Mexico although not impossible. It meant she would be on the run again.

This whole plan of Jeronimo's was spinning out of control. She wondered if there was any way she could convince Jeronimo to call it all off? She doubted it. She sat there shuffling through her options. There was no way she would run without Jaime.

And she couldn't in good faith abandon Jeronimo, at least not without telling him what the Fed had just revealed.

She brooded for a minute before picking up her cell phone and punching in Jeronimo's number. She allowed it to ring a dozen times before disconnecting. She hesitated a few moments before dialing Jaime's' number. Same thing. Six, seven, eight rings before she disconnected.

Why weren't either of them picking up? She would just have to wait for Jaime to leave and then try them both again.

Chapter 18

Jaime paused and scanned the street in each direction. As he drove up, he had taken note of the Penske rental truck parked down the street. He adjusted his rear view mirror and thought he saw someone sitting in the van's driver's seat.

The only pedestrian he noticed was a woman pushing a baby stroller and dressed in a loose-fitting dress and a baseball cap. It appeared she had paused to talk on her cell phone. There were several cars parked down the street, but they were too far away to see if they were occupied. He was sure however that someone was watching.

Jeronimo had called an hour before to suggest he come to the hotel. There had been no further communication from either Vera or Becerra. At this point, he had no way of calling them. He could only assume that Becerra knew where Jeronimo would be staying, and that Jaime would at some point go there.

Vera, if that was her real name, had been coy about disclosing any real details about Becerra's specific intentions which meant he was still flying blind without any formulation of a plan.

After Vera left, he briefly contemplated calling Lilly and at least assure her that he was okay. He could be sure that Lilly was angry and worried. Twice this morning, she had called without leaving a message.

Something told him that in spite of his urging Jeronimo to leave Lilly out of this, she would manage to somehow insert herself. He knew she would wheedle it out of the old man. Jeronimo seemed to be increasingly unable to resist Lilly's entreaties. The two of them had developed an interesting relationship, one that resembled more of a father and his headstrong daughter. Jaime hoped that for once Jeronimo would be able to resist her interrogation.

He hurried through the lobby to the rear of the hotel and made his way to the private bungalow situated in the gardens just beyond the conservatory. Flowerbeds containing native wild flowers lined the pathway. Hummingbird feeders hung from every available branch of the live oaks dotting the property.

He paused to stare at a security camera nestled in the one of the trees branches. When he had been at the hotel two weeks ago, he had discovered that for some unexplained reason the cameras had all been disconnected. He wondered if his demand they be turned back on had been heeded. It would be something to check.

As he approached the cottage, Ernesto pushed up awkwardly from a chaise lounge beside the door. He waited for Jaime with his arms flung open in greeting.

"*Amigo,*" he exclaimed, clasping Jaime in a tight embrace.

"Hey, *tu viejo gordo*," Jaime replied affectionately. In spite of the old Mexican's physical limitations, Jaime wasn't at all surprised by Jeronimo's choice of a bodyguard.

Ernesto released Jaime from his embrace and stepped back and studied him with mock severity. "*Y tu eres la Judas,*" he whispered hoarsely.

"*Asi parece.*" So it would have to seen, Jaime thought. "Let's go see the boss."

Chapter 19

The bungalow was decorated to suit the tastes of someone willing to pay two thousand dollars a night with a five night minimum. It had a large living room, a chef's kitchen and a dining area that would seat eight, two bedrooms and private baths, one of which featured a Jacuzzi. The décor was French provincial with stone walls hung with rather expensive original art work and furniture that had been purchased in a lot from a Parisian foreclosure. The bungalow was comfortable without being pretentious.

Jeronimo sat in a high backed, provincial style chair with a cup of coffee balanced on his knee. He wore his usual daytime attire of a white dress shirt, tailored slacks and house slippers.

"*Comó está,* Jaime," he said, tilting his chin in greeting, He made no effort to rise. He had never been the type for warm embraces. "You look well," he said, nodding for Jaime to take a seat.

Jaime dropped onto a blue velvet divan.

"Before I forget," Jaime said, turning to Ernesto. "Did you find the tools I left you?"

"*Si*, the tools." Ernesto replied. "Do you need one of these tools?"

"No, I already took one of the Glocks." He turned to Jeronimo. "I have to ask this again, boss. What the hell are we doing?"

"You have met with Becerra?"

"Yeah, last night. He's a snake if I ever met one."

"So he is here. He has taken the bait."

"Nibbling," Jaime said.

He recounted the entire encounter beginning with Vera picking him up at the airport, their interlude in the bar, the meeting with Becerra, and ending with the conversation with Vera in the hotel room. He left nothing out. A long silence followed as Jeronimo sipped his coffee.

"What do you make of this Vera woman?" he asked finally.

"Part of me wants to believe her story. But I can't discount the possibility that she's playing me. Testing me. I'm worried that she's reporting back to Becerra everything I say."

Jeronimo finished his coffee and set his cup on a side table "First, you must realize Becerra has no intention of discussing this with his superiors, for they know nothing about his being here. He is merely buying time. And he has no intention of blowing up my car or… What is it called? A drive-by shooting? No, he knows the cartel wishes to keep a low profile here. He intends that I simply disappear into an unmarked grave. He has set a trap, but we have set our own."

"So if I'm going to play act, I'd sure like to get a peek at the script,"

"Very well. I wish for you to continue your play acting. Yes, it would be wonderful if you can discover when and how he plans to move on me. I doubt he will attempt anything here at the hotel. But one never knows. What is more important is to discover his location. Then it will be a simple matter of alerting the proper authorities. Do you believe this Vera when she says she does not know his whereabouts?"

Jaime shrugged. "It makes sense that he would move around and not stay in the same place for long. He's cautious, paranoid is how Vera put it. She said she only communicates with him by phone. So it's going to be hard to find him. Unless I can set up a meeting with him at some prearranged location. But I doubt he'll go for something like that."

"I agree. But we still must draw him out. When will you see Vera again?"

"I don't know. She seems eager to put some kind of plan in action. Let's just say she's pretty motivated to be rid of Becerra."

"Perhaps I should invite Becerra to a meeting."

"Wouldn't that be giving a lot away? I mean, how do we explain you knowing he's here?"

"Simple. You will confess to him that you have told me that he is here"

"Shit, boss. Why in God's name would I tell him that? Are you trying to get me killed? He's going to think I'm more duplicitous than he first thought."

"You will explain it by saying this is the simplest way you are giving me up to him. You will say that you told me you were approached by someone from Jalisco who wishes to make a deal with me regarding my holdings in Mexico City. And that

I have expressed interest in meeting personally to discuss this. He will not guess that I know of his intentions. Remember, he is not aware that I know his true identity."

Jaime nodded. "That might work if he gets to pick the time and place for this meeting."

"My sources tell me that he is cautious, but also at times quite is impetuous. And overly confident. I believe he will agree to such a meeting."

"I don't know, boss. I still think it'll be a hard sell."

A cell phone on the coffee table chirped. Ernesto picked it up and glanced at the screen. He stood and showed Jeronimo the screen. Jeronimo held up his hand as if to signal not now.

After Ernesto settled back into his seat, Jeronimo looked over at him. Ernesto had been uncharacteristically quiet through all this discussion.

¿Qué te parece, amigo?" Jeronimo asked him.

"I think if Jaime can find him, you should allow me take care of him. There is no need for *la chota* or *la DEA.*"

Jeronimo offered him one of his rare smiles. "We are not in *Ciudad de México, amigo.* And it is not like it was in the old days."

"Yes, we are old dogs. But I can still bite."

"Si. No lo dudo. Pero...

Jaime's phone rang. He glanced at it and saw it was Lilly. He disconnected and set it on the divan beside him.

"Do you have a way of contacting Vera?" Jeronimo asked Jaime.

"No, but I have a feeling she's not going to waste much time getting back to me."

"You will ask to speak to Becerra, or at least ask her if she can arrange a meeting. It is important that we find out the location ahead of time. But I doubt we will be so fortunate."

"It's going to be a bit of a balancing act with Vera. She still thinks that I want you dead, and if she helps me, then I'll be obligated to help her with Becerra. Let's just hope she doesn't get overeager and takes it upon herself to kill you without me knowing."

Jeronimo pointed his thumb at Ernesto. "She does not know about my dog."

Jaime rose to his feet. "I better make myself available. I'll let you know as soon as I hear from her."

"There is one other thing you should know. Lilia is here. Watching."

"God…" He held his tongue. "I asked you to leave her out of this."

"And did you really think she would stay away? It is better to have her here than not. Do you not agree?"

"No, I don't agree. So where is she?"

"Watching."

"Is she armed?"

"Ernesto just left a package for her at the front desk. I have instructed her to remain in the background. To be our eyes only."

"Sure. Whatever you say," Jaime said, not bothering to conceal his irritation. "I'll set up the meet," he said and turned to leave.

Ernesto followed him out the door. Jaime turned and looked at him

"Things could easily go wrong here. *Estás de acuerdo?* You know? I'm just not buying this plan. Someone is going to get killed."

"Who is it you worry about, *amigo? El jefe?Ernesto.? Tú?* No, you worry about Lilia. *¿Si?*"

"Just promise me you'll keep her away from this."

"*Prometo* I will try, *pero ella es muy teerco. Obstinada.*"

"That she is. And she doesn't know when she should be afraid. Do you know where she is?"

"*En el parque, creo.* Watching. I see her sitting on *un banco.* That was she who called while we talked."

"I'll call you as soon as I know something," he said and walked to his car.

Chapter 20

Jaime went back to his car and checked the street. The Penske rental truck was still there. One car remained parked on the street a block or so down from the hotel. He got in his car and pulled into the drive. That was when he saw her then walking in the direction of the hotel. Did he dare stop and run the risk of possibly blowing her cover?

As he drew closer, he could tell she had taken notice of him. As he passed slowly by her, he gave her a quick sidelong glance. She did the same. He drove a couple of blocks, pulled over, and called her.

"What the hell are you doing?" he asked when she picked up.

"I could ask you the same thing."

"I knew Jeronimo wasn't going to be able to keep you out of this. He said you're supposed to stay in the background. You do that. You hear me? No flying off the handle or cowboy shit like you did in Houston," he said, referring to the time they tried to buy a couple of Glocks from a Jamaican guy who made the mistake of attempting to double cross them. When the attempted rip off became obvious, Lilly had reacted by almost killing the Jamaican, and revealing to Jaime a side of her that worried him.

"There're some things you need to know," she said, ignoring his chastisement. . "First off, that Penske van down the street. It's the Feds and they're watching Jeronimo. They know about you, too."

"What do you mean?"

"One of them was kind enough to come up to me and tell me. Shit, Jaime. The jig is up and Jeronimo needs to call this off."

"I already tried to talk him out of it. No go."

"This Fed also said you were consorting, his words not mine, with a woman who's a hitter for the Jalisco cartel. What the fuck, *güero?*"

Vera. A cartel hitter? That suddenly made sense. He let the silence build before he said anything.

"Look, this is all going to be over in twenty- four hours at most. In the meantime, you stay low. Don't get involved. Will you promise me you'll do that? Lilly? Did you hear what I said?"

"We need to talk, Jaime," she said, filling the silence.

"Yeah, we do. Look, I've been thinking. We can't go on like this."

"You're dumping me. Is that it?"

"Shit, no. That's not what I meant. Listen…"

"It's okay. I'm not who you think I am. I've done things."

He laughed. "I know what you've done. About your past. You don't think Jeronimo would've told me before we partnered up?"

"Fuck Jeronimo."

"Where's this coming from? I thought we were solid."

"We are," she said after a moment of silence. "At least I hope so. I just can't do this anymore. Run Jeronimo's fucked up errands. I'm tired of us putting our lives on the line. Or both of us traveling so much."

"I hear you. I almost just told Jeronimo to stuff it. That I was done. What I guess I'm saying is I want a normal life. Lilly," he said when she didn't say anything.

"I'm here."

"How about I sneak into your room tonight and we talk about it?"

"Too risky. Too many people watching. How about we just meet in a parking lot somewhere and do some heavy petting?"

"Lord, I wish. Like I said, the chances are this will be over pretty quick. Then I'll take you up on the heavy petting."

"Promise?"

"I love you, Lilly. Just please don't take any unnecessary risks. No cowboying."

"Where are you off to?"

"I have to try to set up a meeting between Jeronimo and Becerra. Or at least try to nail down his whereabouts."

"Be careful. I love you, güero. "

"I love you, too. Call me before you go to sleep," he said and disconnected.

Chapter 21

She began walking back to the hotel. To her surprise, she saw the woman who earlier had been pushing the baby stroller walking in her direction. At least, she thought it was the same woman for she was no longer pushing the stroller. She looked different, too. Gone was the loose-fitting smock as well as the baseball cap. Instead, she wore a pair of tight denim jeans, a black T-shirt, bright red low-heeled sandals, and a straw fedora. She still wore the same over-sized mirrored sun glasses.

"*Hola,*" the woman said as she drew near.

"*Hola,*" Lilly replied as the two of them stopped a few feet apart. "*¿Donde esta la bebe?*" Lilly asked.

"She is not my baby. I watch her. Baby sit," she said in halting, heavily-accented English.

Lilly nodded. When the woman didn't say anything else, Lilly asked, "Do you have a child? Your own children?"

"*No más.* No more," the woman replied evenly after a moment of hesitation.

Lilly felt unsure as to what to say other than "I'm sorry. *Lo siento.*"

"*¿Habla español?*"

"*Un poco..*"

For some reason, Lilly didn't want to give away the fact she was fluent.

"I had a child. *Una vez.*" The woman gave Lilly a look that was half smile and half grimace. "Someone take her from me." The woman's accent suddenly seemed less obvious and tentative. The two women stared at each for an uncomfortable moment.

"I was going to my room," Lilly said, pointing at the hotel and hoping to cut short their conversation.

The woman only nodded. Lilly smiled and started to walk away when the woman said, "You wait for him. You are his woman. ¿Si?"

Lilly stopped and stared at the woman. Something about this whole encounter suddenly felt way off. Her initial confusion quickly pivoted to what Jaime once referred to her 'fully loaded and cocked' mind set.

"Who are you?"

The woman didn't answer.

"Look, if you're trying to tell me something, why don't you cut the bullshit and just tell me. Who are you? An undercover cop? Or are you…" Lilly asked, suddenly remembering what the Fed had told her. Was this the woman? The hitter?

The woman lowered her sunglasses and a grim smile creased the woman's fac.

"*No polis. Pero,* I see things. I know things. *No soy una bruja.* I am not a witch if that is what you think. Or some crazy woman. No."

Something in the tone of the woman's voice or perhaps it was the smile that led Lilly to suspect the woman was toying with her. And what was the reason for her approaching Lilly?

It suddenly occurred to her that it was becoming increasingly more difficult to keep track of the various teams. Cops, Feds, Becerra's people, Becerra's enemies, the various competing cartels. This woman could be with any of them.

The woman stared at Lilly intently, as if attempting to read her thoughts. Her eyes were slightly slanted with dark brown pupils and crazy long eyelashes,

"I tell you," she said finally. "I know things before they happen. Your man, you tell him the rabbit must always be looking for *la trampa.* The trap. Tell him he needs help. He will understand this.'

She brushed past Lilly and walked down the street in the direction of the park. It took all of Lilly's reserve to keep from hurrying after the woman and attempting to get the truth out of her. One thing Lilly could be sure of was that someone besides the Feds had made her. But to what end? She watched the woman disappear around the corner. She needed to talk to Jeronimo, she thought as she hurried back to the hotel.

Chapter 22

When Jaime returned to his room he wasn't at all surprised to find a voice mail from Vera. All it said was that Becerra had agreed to Jaime's terms and to call her. She picked up on the first ring.

"Tell him Hermosa wants a face to face meeting," he said, forgoing any pleasantries.

There was a long silence before she replied. "That is… surprising. *No comprednio. ¿Como…*"

"Just see if you can set it up. I'll explain it to you later."

"*Muy bien,* I will tell him. And have you thought about what we talked about?"

"I'll have to see how things play out. Call me and tell me when and where. Okay?"

She replied with a simple *si* and hung up. Twenty minutes later, she called back.

"Licha's Cantina on East 6th. Eight o'clock tomorrow night. I hope you know what you do," she said and hung up before he could reply.

"Yeah, me, too," he muttered.

He called Ernesto and relayed the name of the place and the time. After he hung up, he checked to see if the mini-bar had been restocked and laid down for a nap, but too many things ran through his mind. Paramount of which was how to keep Lilly on the sidelines. He was worried it was out of his hands and now up to Jeronimo. He fell asleep ruminating on the prospect of Lilly gumming up the plan.

Chapter 23

Ernesto answered Jeronimo's phone with a curt *Sí*.

"It's Lilia. Where is he?"

"*Él está durmiendo.*"

"Then wake him up. I need to talk to him."

When Ernesto didn't say anything, she went on. "The Penske van down the street. *Es Federales.*"

"*Sí,* we know that."

All she could think of was that Jaime must have noticed the van and told them.

"There is also a woman who walks and watches. She knows something. I think she might work for Becerra."

"*Esta mujer. Una Mexicana?*"

"Yeah. How did you know?"

"I only guess."

"Bullshit. Come on, Ernesto. Tell me what's going on."

She heard him sigh. "Okay, I tell you. Becerra has a woman that works for him. She says she wishes to betray him. She tells this to Jaime."

"And he fucking believes her? This is turning into a shit show."

"Shit show. I like that. I like learning your *gabacho jerga*. This … describes everything very well. *Si.* A shit show."

"Ernesto. I need to speak with Jeronimo."

"When he wakes up, I tell him to call you. Okay?"

"You do that."

"Did you get your package?" he asked just as she was about to disconnect.

"Yeah, I did. Tell him to call."

She fell back onto the bed and stared at the ceiling for a moment before reaching on the bed beside her for the package wrapped in brown paper. She could guess what it was. She sat up and flipped the lid off the Adidas shoe box and brushed away the tissue paper to reveal the handgun and a couple of full clips.

She didn't know if this made her feel better or worse. It had been over a year since she had held a weapon or had any intent to use one. That life was behind her she kept telling herself. But she had made her bed so to speak by placing her fortunes in the employ of one Jeronimo Hermosa. No more of this, she had told both herself and Jeronimo on more than one occasion. And didn't Jaime try to keep her away from this latest shit show? She had no one to blame but herself.

She was hungry. The hotel restaurant was still closed ever since the staff had walked out two weeks ago. It was partially the reason why the hotel sat half-empty. She picked up the takeout and delivery folder from the nightstand. Upset stomach be damned. She called a Thai restaurant on South Congress and ordered *pad thai* with green mango salad extra spicy, and then sat back to wait for Jeronimo to call.

Chapter 24

Following Becerra's text message Vera waited at the Four Season's entrance. It was beginning to get dark, and the sidewalk was crowded with what she assumed were spectators returning from observing the dusk bat swarm. She had hurried back downtown from Hermosa's hotel, her mind racing as she attempted to formulate a plan on the fly. Should she kill them both? Hermosa and Miguel? And would Soledad help her?

She couldn't be sure yet whether she could depend on Soledad for she sensed a degree of ambivalence regarding his fervor to betray Hermosa. Was it merely cold feet on his part or was there some element of duplicity that she was missing?

All she knew was that she wanted to return to a normal life, not that she had ever had experienced such a thing. Earlier that afternoon, she had observed the mothers and their children playing in the park. The pain of witnessing people going about their daily life without fear of the ever present specter of violence and uncertainty was at times soul crushing.

She thought again about her encounter with the woman who she was certain was Soledad's woman. If so, how was she involved in all this? On the surface, the woman seemed to simply be watching the comings and goings at the hotel. But to what end? Was she helping Soledad in his plot to rid them of Hermosa? She couldn't be sure of anything anymore.

The sound of a car honking interrupted her thoughts. An Escalade SUV pulled into the hotel drive. The rear window lowered, and she leaned over and saw Becerra in the back seat. She opened the door and started to get in, but he hissed.

"*Al frente,*" he said, nodding with his head for her to sit in front.

She got in, and the driver pulled out onto San Jacinto Boulevard and headed in the direction of Congress Avenue. The driver was somebody different than the driver she was familiar with, although his vigilance in constantly checking the rear mirrors was no different. They crossed over the river on Congress Avenue before turning onto the parkway that paralleled the river. After a couple of blocks, the driver pulled over into a small parking lot and cut the ignition

"*Como dijiste, fue al hotel Heromosas.,*" she said, without bothering to turn.

"English," Becerra said with obvious irritation.

She turned in her seat to face him and waited for him to say something. He leaned into his cigarette lighter, the flame momentarily illuminating his face.

"You have seen Soledad?" he asked

"I watched him go into Hermosa's hotel."

He paused to take a couple of long drags on his cigarette before saying anything. "I no longer have any use for him. You will deal with him. Tonight."

"And Hermosa?"

"I will deal with him." He took another pull of his cigarette and flicked it out the window. "Tomorrow, we return to Guadalajara."

She felt a wave of panic. Tomorrow? She planned on having at least a day to pull this off. She fumbled for something to say. Once they returned to Mexico, it would only prove more difficult to do anything.

"You are sure you can deal with Hermosa tonight? Perhaps, if we wait another…"

"No. You will do what I tell you to do. Hermosa is my problem. ¿Lo *entiendes?*" he asked, his voice dripping with venom.

She realized then he no longer trusted her. Obviously he didn't trust her enough for her to join him in the rear seat. She knew in that moment that she was not meant to survive the night. Just like Soledad, she had worn out her usefulness.

She lifted her bag onto her lap. The switchblade was concealed in an open side pocket. Would she have the time to grasp it, lunge across the seat and stab him? Or would it be better to take out the driver first? If Becerra was armed, she doubted she would have the time or opportunity to kill them both.

In her mind's eye, she visualized the knife slashing across Becerra's throat, just as she had once done to one of his rivals as they lay together naked in bed. The only other time she had killed for him it had merely required her to hold a pillow over the face of a drunken police commander whose services Becerra no longer required.

Entertaining any possibility that she would be able to kill Miguel before they returned to Mexico was beginning to seem increasingly remote. Her only hope was to convince Soledad to help her. But first they would have to locate Miguel before the night was over. But how would that be possible without knowing his plan? She would have to know his every move.

Of course, how stupid of me, she thought as she suddenly remembered something. Miguel had provided her with a GPS tracking device to place on Soledad's car. Something she had never gotten around to doing. It was still in her purse.

She glanced at the driver who seemed to be more engaged in checking his rear view mirrors than watching her. As surreptitiously as possible, she reached into her bag and gingerly fumbled for the small device, all the while watching the driver out of the corner of her eye. He didn't seem to notice. She lifted her bag to conceal her movements, and carefully switched the tracker on and slipped it into the door's side pocket.

She turned back to face Becerra. "Do you have a gun I can use? I may need it."

He stared at her in the dimness, his eyes betraying nothing. "You will use your knife. It has served you well before" he said, "Do it tonight. I will call you and we will come and get you. ¿Lo *entiendes?*" Becerra tapped the driver on the shoulder. "*Llévala de regreo al hotel,*"

She turned back in her seat. She knew what that meant. She had to somehow convince Soledad to help her.

Chapter 25

Jaime awoke to a knock on his door. He squinted at the clock on the night stand. It was almost seven and the room had grown dim. The knock again. He swung his legs over the side of the bed and switched on the bedside lamp before walking to the door and peering through the peek hole. Vera. He opened the door, but he made no effort to invite her in.

She stood there holding a bottle in a paper sack. In the other hand, she clutched what appeared to be a plastic bag containing a Styrofoam takeout carton which she held out to him.

"*Barbacoa de cabra. Frijoles negra, y plántanos con miel,*" she said, somberly.

"Beware of strangers bearing gifts," he muttered.

"*¿Qué?* "

She wore the same slinky, strapless black cocktail dress she had worn in the bar the night before. No wig this time, her black hair grazing her bare shoulders. She wore no lipstick, and it appeared she made an effort to wipe away her eye makeup.

"Were you looking for me in the bar?" he asked.

"*Es* better I come here. Too many eyes in the bar."

Her voice sounded slurred and he could smell liquor on her breath. She had the kind of loopy look on her face brought on by too many shots of tequila.

He took the takeout carton from her and nodded with his head for her to come in. He placed the carton on the nightstand. Without waiting for an invitation, she slipped her purse from her shoulder and dropped into a chair. She waited a moment before lifting the bottle of brown liquor from the paper sack to show him. It appeared to be half-empty.

"I do not think your room is bugged," she said, pulling the stopper from the bottle. "One of Miguel's men checked. So we can talk freely. *Por favor,*" she said, handing him the bottle and offering him one of those smiles you only see in funeral parlors.

He pulled up a chair and poured them each a drink and handed her a glass. She downed hers without the slightest hesitation.

"I see Miguel tonight. He tells me we go back to Mexico tomorrow. After he kills Hermosa," she added.

"He plans to kill Hermosa tonight?"

She shrugged. "Mebbe. Tell me, why does Hermosa wish for this meeting?"

"I don't know. Maybe he's trying make peace. Maybe give Becerra a piece of his Mexico City operation."

"It is too late for that. To make such an agreement."

She lifted her glass and then realized it was empty. He held out the bottle but she shook her head.

"You still don't know where he's staying?"

"No," she replied after a moment's hesitation.

She's lying, he thought. But why? She held out her glass out again. He topped it off, hoping the tequila might loosen her tongue.

"I must find Alma. *Mi hija.* He tol' me once she is in *el convent. ¿Pero donde?* He tells me he is taking her away from the convent. *¿Donde?* To where? He will not tell me. He does this to… *comtrolame.* To control me. To make me do everything but open my legs for him."

She took a deep breath and looked at him before going on.

"I was once his whore. His whore," she said, looking away. "I have also slept with his enemies. Betrayed many friends." She seemed to disappear somewhere for a moment. "I have killed for him. *Si,* I do this," she said in reaction to his look of mild surprise. She laughed softly. "Yes, I come here tonight to kill you. This is what he wishes for me to do."

Chapter 26

Jaime allowed his eyes to drop to the purse at her side. His Glock was under his pillow. He calculated his chances. If she had a gun in her purse, would he be able to vault across the bed and to get his gun before she could reach hers? Then again, she was drunk. She studied him, her expression unrevealing.

The sound of his cell phone chirping in the nightstand broke the silence. He let it ring and go to voice mail, his eyes never leaving hers.

"Your food. *Es* going to become cold," she said her voice level.

"Are you going to join me?"

"No. I have eaten. Go on," she said, nodding with her chin at the carton on the bed.

He wondered what kind of game she was playing. He paused a moment before picking up the carton and opening it. She could have poisoned it, he thought, lifting the food to his nose to smell it. It sure as hell looked appetizing. How could she have known he loved barbecued goat?

"No. I do not poison you if this is what you think," she said, downing half of her glass of tequila. "I will not kill you. *Al menos,* not tonight. Mebe some other time," she, offering a drunken grin.

"What do you want, Vera?" he asked, fishing a plastic fork from the bag.

"I must kill him before we go back to Mexico."

"And before you kill him, you're going to make him tell you where your daughter is?"

"I no longer need him for that. I just do not want him returning to Mexico."

He took a bite of the *barbacoa.* It was quite good.

"My father liked to barbecue goat. We had this ranch in South Texas. Just across the Rio Grande. Shitty land. Just scrub and mesquite. When the old man couldn't afford to buy cattle feed anymore, he started raising goats. We ate a lot of goat."

He licked his fingers as they both watched each other. She was back in her chameleon skin. The seductress again - all easy limbed and open faced, her lips parted.

"And how exactly do you plan on doing this? Killing him?" he asked through another a mouthful of goat.

"You will help me. Yes? "

"I'm not agreeing to anything. Not yet. There has to be another way to get rid of him. Why not just tell the Feds where he is? I'm sure they can find some reason to hold him."

"I tol' you. I do not know where he is. Besides, your Federals will do nothing. You must understand that Miguel is a very careful man. If they arrest him, he will know who betrays him."

"What if you wait until his own people deal with him?"

"What do you mean? The Jalisco?"

"It could happen. I hear he's ambitious, and wants to take over. I'm betting he has enemies. Maybe if you told someone. Warned them. They might move on him first."

"There is no time for that." She paused before going on. "I cannot allow him to return to Mexico. All things must be done tonight."

"Like killing me?"

She shrugged. "*Tal vez.*'"

He stood and placed the food carton on the bed and sat down beside it, his pillow and the Glock in easy reach.

"Look, if you know anything about this hit on Hermosa, tell me now. I just need to be clear of it. Or does he expect you to do it?"

She took another drink. "Do you still want your boss…. *muerto*" She made a swiping motion across her throat. "¿Si? For this woman? You know I see her. The woman with the limp. This afternoon I even speak with her."

Jaime paused just as he started to take a swallow of his tequila, his mind tumbling over how he might respond. Plead ignorance and deny that he knew Lilly was here? For some reason, he didn't think that would work. Vera knew something, knew about Lilly.

"Where did you see her?"

"At Hermosa's hotel. She was watching. She saw you. I wonder what she will do. *¿Sabes?* No? I think you do not know this. What she will do. In Mexico, we call such a thing *la carta aún no jugada.* The card not yet played. Yes? "

That was exactly what it was. The wild card. Both of them. She and Lilly both. This whole thing was out of control. Jeronimo's plan now seemed like a mere side show.

"She came here to help me," he said. "I told her not to. What can I say? She can be… *desobediente"* He looked at her. "If you kill Miguel first, where does that leave me and my boss?"

"We do this together. Kill them both. Tonight."

"I told you. I'm not agreeing to anything yet. Killing Hermosa won't be easy. He doesn't leave the hotel and he has a bodyguard. Besides, I thought Miguel was taking care of that. Listen, you have to tell me before you do anything. Okay?"

"You forget, Jaime. You are in my debt. I have not killed you. And I have not harmed your woman. Miguel no longer trusts me. I believe he wishes to kill me. *Esta noche también"*

They were all a nest of snakes, he thought. And he wasn't sure when or where to step to avoid getting bit.

"So, I'm asking you again. Do you have any idea how you're going to do this?"

Her face darkened and she didn't reply, but instead she slowly lifted her wrist and glanced at her watch. That there was something she wasn't telling him.

"I must go," she said, finishing her drink. "I will call you. Enjoy your *barbacoa.*" She rose and started for the door.

"Vera."

She turned and looked at him. There was what looked to be defeat registered in not only her face, but in the way she held herself. It was as if she had just stared into some horrible abyss and knew there was no retreating from its edge.

"Don't do anything stupid," he said for lack of anything better to say. "Call me."

She nodded an inch and walked out the door. He reached for his phone to check to see who had called. Lilly again, but she hadn't left a message. He punched in Jeronimo's number. He picked up on the second ring.

"Yes, Jaime."

"I think he's going to make a move on you tonight."

There was a moment of silence. "The woman told you this?"

"Yes. She says Becerra plans on going back to Mexico tomorrow."

"Do you believe her?"

"This time, yes. If he's going to do it tonight, he'll be coming for you there. You'd better be ready."

"*Muy bien.*"

"Where's Lilly?"

"I assume in her room."

"I'm coming over. Tell Ernesto not to shoot me," he said and hung up.

He tried calling Lilly, but it went to voice. He grabbed the Glock from beneath his pillow and hurried out the door.

Chapter 27

Lilly grew increasingly irritated that Jeronimo hadn't called her back, but she knew that was his way and there was no point forcing the issue. And why wasn't Jaime picking up? He was probably consorting with the hit woman. Goddamn him.

Her thoughts were interrupted by the Thai food delivery person calling from downstairs. Lilly grabbed her purse and went down. A young Asian woman bearing some cartons in a plastic bag waited just inside the front door. Lilly paid her, leaving her a generous tip before turning back into the lobby. She noticed that the older Hispanic female receptionist wasn't at her usual station behind the desk.

Lilly started up the stairs and then hesitated. She wanted to ask the receptionist if it was possible to grab a beer from the kitchen refrigerator. She went back to the desk and waited a moment before tapping the bell, but no one responded. She doubted anyone would mind if she just helped herself, she thought as she slipped through a side door into the darkened dining room.

It was only then she noticed the door to the office stood ajar. Maybe the receptionist was in there. Lilly rapped softly on the door.

"Excuse me," she said when she didn't receive an answer. She opened the door a few inches and peered around the corner.

The first thing she noticed was a pair of bare legs protruding from behind the desk. The ankles appeared to be bound by what might have been a white tablecloth. The next thing she noticed was the uniformed security guard slumped over and face down on the desk. The dim blue light coming from the computer monitor allowed her to see the dark stain pooling on the newspaper spread on the desk beneath his head.

"Shit, shit," she whispered. She leaned over the edge of the desk and saw the receptionist on the floor, her arms also bound and her mouth taped shut.

Lilly knelt beside her and placed her fingers on the woman's neck. She was alive but unconscious. Lilly placed the carton of food on the desk and tiptoed back to the open office door. If someone was waiting in the darkened dining room, she was surely fucked. She had to get to her room and get her gun and her phone.

She kneeled down beside the security guard and fumbled at his waist. She couldn't recall if she had even seen him before, much less if he had been armed. There was nothing on his belt except a holster containing a flashlight and what she thought might be can of Mace. She pocketed the Mace and peered again over the edge of the desk at the doorway.

It was only then she noticed the screen of the computer monitor. It displayed a grid of small black and white images

– two images of the lobby, another showing the front porch and the drive, and another half dozen more images of the grounds. She squinted at the dim images, but saw nothing out of the ordinary. Just as she was about to turn away, she caught a glimpse of movement on the screen that showed the walkway leading to Jeronimo's bungalow. A shadowy figure stood amongst some shrubs.

She needed to warn them. There had to be something on the desk – an intercom, a phone, some way of contacting the bungalow, but she didn't see any such device. She didn't dare turn on the desk lamp. Creeping out into the darkened dining room, she paused momentarily at the entrance to the lobby. It appeared empty. She again considered seeing if there might be an intercom or a cell phone at the desk, but in the end decided it too risky. Instead, she bolted for the stairs,

When she reached the top of the landing, she was startled by an elderly woman in a bath robe holding an ice bucket.

"Ma'm," Lilly said, doing her best to sound calm. "It's best if you go to your room and lock the door. There's an incident downstairs. Go on, Hurry."

"What kind of incident?" the woman asked.

"Just go. I'll let you know when you can come out."

The woman shrugged and walked back down the hallway.

Lilly hurried into her room, grabbed her phone and punched in Jeronimo's number. He picked up on the first ring.

"They're here," she said before he could even answer."I'm not sure how many. I spotted one on the surveillance camera headed your way. I'll call 911."

"No, wait."

"Wait? For what? They already killed the security guard."

She heard him mutter something unintelligible to Ernesto, followed by the sound of his breathing. She moved to the window facing the front street and looked down the block to see if the Penske van was still there, but it was gone.

"Boss, there's no time. We should call…"

She heard the loud boom of what sounded like the report of a shotgun over the phone. And then a volley of small arms fire.

"Shit!" She grabbed the Glock from the dresser and ran out the door.

Chapter 28

As she reached the upper landing, she could hear the faint staccato echo of another volley of gunfire. She vaulted down the steps three at a time, and had just reached the bottom landing, when her phone rang. She quickly glanced at the screen. It was Jaime.

"They're here!" she gasped, short of breath. "Call the cops and get over here."

"Lilly…"

"Gotta go!" She stuffed the phone in her jeans and ran in a half- crouch to the lobby's front door. She took a moment to scan the porch, and satisfied it was empty, pivoted out the door, down the steps, and started running down the path leading to the rear of the grounds and Jeronimo's bungalow.

Giving into caution, she veered off the pathway, hugging the tree line and shrubs as she allowed her eyes to adjust to the darkness. The gunfire seemed to have stopped. And then she heard a shout and voices coming from the direction of the bungalow. She crouched behind a large live oak tree and waited. The porch light of the bungalow still shone brightly, revealing the open front door.

A few seconds later, three figures emerged. One of them she realized was Jeronimo. The left sleeve of his white dress appeared to be soaked in blood. A figure dressed in black behind him shoved him forward almost sending Jeronimo to his knees. They were heading her way. Where was Ernesto?

She had never considered herself much of a marksman. Firing at a target the size of a pickup truck with a sniper rifle from fifty yards away as she had done in Sonora was one thing. The same could be said for shooting someone in the back from three feet away as she once done in Idaho while saving Harlan Quist's life. But dropping a shadowy, moving and armed target, much less two of them, from twenty yards away with a handgun was an entirely different matter.

She took aim at the man standing behind Jeronimo and squeezed off two rounds. The man lurched backwards, the shotgun discharging harmlessly into the porch's floor. The other man froze for just long enough for Lilly to get off two more shots, but she obviously missed for the man ducked and pivoted, firing off a couple of rounds in Lilly's direction.

Just as she started to shift position in order to get a clear shot, she felt something press hard into the back of her head.

"No te muevas," someone behind her yelled, and her Glock was ripped from her grip. She started to turn and someone struck her in the back of her neck, stunning her. Two pair of hands dragged her roughly to her feet.

"Tráela!" a voice behind her barked.

Someone shoved her to the ground and pressed her face into the dirt. She winced in pain as her arms were wrenched tightly behind her. And then someone kicked her in the head and then there was only darkness.

Chapter 29

Jaime swung around the corner and immediately slammed on the brakes. A phalanx of police cruisers blocked the street, the strobe of their red emergency lights casting an eerie light on the houses on either side of the street.

He knew immediately that he had arrived too late. A cop in the street motioned with her flashlight for him to move to the side. The blare of a siren behind him startled him. It took him a few seconds to react and pull to the curb so the ambulance could squeeze by.

He cut the ignition, and before getting out, stuffed his Glock under the seat. A large group of onlookers had already begun forming on the lawns edging the street. He nudged his way to the front of the crowd. From this distance, it was difficult to see anything. He took out his phone and punched in Lilly's number. A man's voice answered after a few rings.

"Yes, may I help you?" the man said.

"Who is this?" Jaime asked. In the ensuing silence, he could hear other voices in the background followed by the short whoop of the ambulance's siren.

"Sir, would you please identify yourself?: the voice asked,

Jaime hung up and looked around. Where the hell was Lilly? If they had her phone that meant... What?

"Goddammit!"

He stood gazing at the chaotic scene before him. There were a couple of what appeared to be SWAT team cops holding assault rifles and smoking cigarettes. A female cop shepherded an elderly woman in a bath robe to a parked cruiser. And two EMS buses parked in the hotel drive.

Jaime turned to a woman standing next to him. "Do you know what happened?" he asked her.

"Not exactly. I heard it though. A bunch of what must've been gunshots. Then some cars tearing out of the hotel's drive. I didn't come out until I heard the cop sirens. Must've been no matter than a minute or two later."

He had called 911 as he weaved through the congested evening traffic on Congress Avenue, but obviously it was too late. He walked toward the barricade of parked police cruisers in the off chance one of the cops would talk to him.

He went up to an uniformed female cop wearing a Kevlar vest and cradling a shotgun. She held up a hand to stop him.

"Please, officer. My wife. She works at the hotel she doesn't answer her phone. Look, I used to be on the job. Just tell me what happened."

The cop turned to look at something happening behind her. Jaime could see the ambulance attendants loading a stretcher onto the bus. All he could make out was that the figure on the stretcher wore an oxygen mask that concealed any appreciation of who it might be. Through the mass of bodies, he caught a quick glimpse of another stretcher at the edge of the driveway. It held a zipped up body bag.

"Please. Just tell me what happened," he pleaded, attempting to sound appropriately distraught.

"Look, sir. Your wife is probably safe."

"What do you mean probably?'

"I'm sorry. You'll have to wait..."

"Just tell me. Was a woman shot?"

The cop hesitated. "No, not a woman. There were two male fatalities. One wounded. Look, that's all I can tell you. Now please move to the side."

He stepped over to the curb as the EMS bus edged through the blockade. As it started to pass by he rushed up beside it and attempted to see into the window.

"Hey!" the cop yelled. "Sir, I thought I told you to step away."

He stepped back on the curb. He couldn't be sure, but it almost looked like it might have been Ernesto on the gurney with an oxygen mask clamped over his face. He turned and began walking back to his car just as his phone chirped again. He looked at the phone, but didn't immediately recognize the number.

"Jaime?" It was Vera.

"What the fuck? Did you know this was happening?"

"I tell you it would be tonight. *¿No lo hice? ¿Qué pasó?*"

He tried to tamp down his anger "Shit, I don't know! There was a shootout here at the hotel. All I know is there are two dead. Both males. I'm guessing Hermosa might be one of them. Lilly…. I don't know where she is. Is there any way you can find out what happened?"

"Miguel will call me, he says. To make sure I killed you. He… *Esperar.* He is calling me now," she said and disconnected.

He leaned against the fender and tried to calm his growing unease. If the cops had Lilly's phone… What did that mean? He began to panic. The phone rang.

"He has them both, Hermosa and your woman."

"Fuck! I have to find them. Goddammit! Vera, if you want Becerra, you're going to help me. You hear me!"

"Do not worry. I have a way. Meet me behind the Four Seasons where I picked you up before."

Chapter 30

Lilly came to in a fitful fog of pain, delirium, and the fetid stench of something burning her nostrils. She gasped and coughed, recoiling at the smell of what she immediately recognized as manure. And something else. An acrid chemical smell. Urine. She tried to twist away, but found she couldn't move her arms or legs. It took a mere few seconds before she realized her hand and feet were tightly bound.

She attempted to open her eyes, but her right eye was swollen shut, the other eye caked with something, blood perhaps. The right side of her face throbbed with pain. And then she remembered being kicked on that side of her head. But that was all she remembered.

She started to raise her head and realized she must have been lying on a bed of straw that felt pasted to the side of her face by the blood she guessed. Squinting with her one good eye she was able to barely make out a faint rectangle of light above her. It was more of just a lessening of the darkness rather than really light.

"*Chica.*" a hoarse, guttural voice croaked from somewhere nearby. "Can you hear me?"

Was she only imagining it? With some effort, she flipped onto her back.

"Who….who's there?"

Someone to her right coughed. "*Soy yo.* Jeronimo. Are you hurt?"

The question elicited a laugh from her that quickly turned into a groan.

"Been better," she managed to say. And worse, she thought, trying to hold back the memory of her captivity in the horse stables in Sonora. She wasn't nearly in that bad of shape. Not yet at least.

"*¿Cómo estás, jefe?*"

"I felt very sure that I was dead until I heard you cough. You are bound?"

"Trussed up like a Christmas turkey."

¿Qué?"

"Do you have any idea where we are?"

"I think in a… *¿Cómo dices?* A horse trailer. The smell."

"I think… I think we are truly fucked," she muttered, rolling back onto her side.

"*Lo siento.* I should have listened to Jaime."

That makes two of us, she thought. They fell silent for perhaps a minute.

"Ernesto," he said. "*Umo valiente*"

"Yes," was all she could manage.

"*Escuchar.* Someone comes."

Sure enough, she could hear what sounded like a vehicle approaching. It seemed to pull up near the rear of the trailer for she could suddenly see light leaking though the louvered ventilation panels on the rear doors.

A moment went by and she could hear voices. Then suddenly the trailer's gates screeched as they were flung open. The bright headlights of the vehicle blinded her and she turned her head away. It was only then that she could make out Jeronimo huddled in the opposite corner.

The trailer rocked slightly as someone stepped inside. She tried to see, but only was able to make out a silhouette partially blocking the headlights. The figure moved towards them and then squatted in front of Jeronimo. The glare of the headlights again made it difficult for Lilly to realize anything of the person's features.

"¿Me *conoces, cabron? No? Estoy aqui para buscar mi venganza. Por Ramon.*"The man cleared his throat and spat his phlegm at Jeronimo. "*Ramón era mi hermano. Pagarás ¿Si?,*" the man said with obvious amusement.

Jeronimo muttered something unintelligible in reply that made the man laugh. "*Un comic. No por mucho tiempo.*"

The man turned and looked at Lilly. "Who are you? Police? Or one of those *Tejanos* always with your gun? "

Lilly considered her answer as she tied to work up enough saliva in her mouth to reply. "Hotel security. Are you the intruder? If so, I must ask you to leave."

"*Otra comic.* You know *puta.* You know you kill one of my men? *No es bueno.*" He rose to his feet, "I have for you…*una gran spreesa.* Big surprise for both of you. I think you will not find it so amusing."

"*Déjala ir,*" Jeronimo croaked.

"No, she must stay. *Sera mas entretenido.*"

The man who she assumed was Becerra turned and left the trailer. A moment passed before someone closed the trailer gates, followed by the slam of a bolt locking into place. A minute or so passed before they heard a vehicle back up to the front of the trailer. She felt the front of the trailer tilt upwards and then heard and felt the clunk of a trailer hitch being dropped into place.

"What do you think they're going to do?" Lilly asked.

"*No sé. Eeee, Lilia. Lo siento.* This is not good." She heard him sigh deeply. "There are things that must be said. *Primero…*" He coughed and cleared his throat. "You have become like a daughter to me. You have brought my granddaughter back to me. You have…"

"Jeronimo. *Suficiente. Por favor.* There is no time for this. Can you move?"

"No. My arm. It is useless. They shot me. We are bound. Any ideas, *chica?* I have been told you have been in worse places."

Worse than this? She was beginning to have her doubts. This was going to end badly. And something told her it wasn't just going to be a bullet in the back of the head.

Giving into her rising panic, she swung her body back and forth, wriggling at the bindings. It was tape of some sort and wasn't giving. She brought her wrist to her mouth and began ripping at the tape with her teeth, but all she managed to accomplish was to fray the edges.

She dropped back and tried to think of a way out of the bindings. Instead, she thought of Jaime and the probability she would never see him again.

Did she ever really think there would be a happy ending somewhere in this? Her life had been nothing but false starts and disappointments. Always look for the pot of gold at the end of the rainbow, her derelict mother used to preach. It was nothing more than a cruel mirage.

Her head banged against the side of the trailer as the vehicle pulling the trailer started off. To where? She struggled to shut from her mind the possibilities for they were all at this moment too terrifying. She took a couple of deep breaths in an effort to calm herself. Just give me the chance. Anything, even if it meant a quick death.

After a moment, the rough, rutted road seemed to give way to smooth pavement. Maybe they would have time. Just maybe. She started again to frantically chew on the tape binding her wrists.

Chapter 31

Other than a couple of delivery vans, the loading docks behind the Four Seasons appeared deserted. Jaime pulled in to a spot between some dumpsters and got out. Vera was nowhere in sight. It had taken no more than fifteen minutes at the most to get here. He was losing precious time. He started to call her when a pickup appeared and pulled up beside him.

"Get in. *Apurarse!*" Vera yelled. "We have not so much time."

Jaime ducked into his car and grabbed the Glock from beneath the seat and piled in beside her. She accelerated before he had even closed the door.

"Where the fuck are they?" he yelled, not at all bothering to conceal his anger.

Vera held up her phone to show him something, but he ignored her.

"For chrissakes, just tell me where we're going."

"I have a phone app that tells me. It tells me where Miguel's car is. I put a tracker in his car."

"And what if he changes cars?" He shook his head in frustration. "Alright, so where's his car?"

"There is a part of town called West Lake Hills. The app says he is there now."

"I know where that is," he said. "Turn here," he said, indicating for her to head towards the Congress Avenue Bridge. "How long has he been there?"

"Ten minutes. He was at another place before. A place that I think looks outside of the city. Not far. Close. But now he is in this West Lake Hills."

"He called you, right? What did he say?"

"He say he has Hermosa. I ask him if he also has Hermosa's bodyguard. He say theoman. And I say what woman? He say the woman who killed one of his men. He asks me then if I have killed you. I tell him yes. He say to wait at the hotel and one of his men will come for me. *Si.* They will come for me," she said in almost a whisper.

She paused at the traffic light before the bridge, looked in both directions, and then accelerated through the intersection, almost running down a cyclist.

"He didn't say if he had killed them already?" he asked, looking at her in the dim reflected light of the oncoming traffic. Would he be able to tell if she would answer truthfully?

"No, *pero…* I did not ask."

"Because you could really give a shit. You just want him. Right? Let me have the phone," he said, trying to rip it from her grasp.

She pulled it away. "We do this together. Find him. And we find your woman."

If it wasn't already too late. She was right. He really had no choice, but to find and confront Becerra. And then what? He didn't want to go there. Not yet.

"Do you have a gun?" he asked.

"No. I only have this," she said, retrieving something her purse. "*Una navaja automatica.* Switchblade, yes? And you?'

"I've got this," he said, showing her the Glock."But no extra clips. And all you've got is a knife? And here I was told you're a hitter."

"Hitter? *¿Qué es eso?*"

"A hit man… woman. *Una asesina*"

"*¿Una asesina?* Who tells you this?"

"Just tell me the truth for a change. Leave out the Alma bullshit. You're here to kill Becerra, aren't you? And Hermosa, too. Am I right?"

She didn't reply.

"I don't like being played."

"And you are not playing? *¿Solo finges?* Pretend."

That was the problem. Everyone was pretending. He, Vera, Jeronimo, Becerra. Even Lilly in the shadows. Duplicity in spades.

"Tell me how many men can we expect Becerra will have with him?"

"*No sé.* He never brings more than three, mebbe four. Your woman, Miguel says she kill one of them. This woman of yours. ¿Ella *es peligrosa?*"

"Yeah, you could say that."

They fell silent as they passed along the river and turned up South Lamar. Fortunately, the traffic was light and it took them only a couple of minutes to turn onto Barton Creek and into Zilker Park.

"Has he moved?"

She turned on her phone and studied the screen. "He is moving," she said. "The map. It shows the river."

"Lake Austin."

"It looks like he is driving on a road that follows the river. This lake."

They left the park and turned onto the exit leading onto the MoPac Freeway. After a short distance, they exited again at the sign to West Lake Hills.

"Be careful. There's a speed limit here. We don't need a cop stopping us," he cautioned her.

If they were stopped, all the explaining in the world probably wouldn't help them. They would only be wasting precious time, if there really was any to waste, he thought ruefully.

He attempted to erase from his mind the likely reason Becerra was driving to the lake. It probably meant he was going somewhere he could dispose of some bodies.

"Let me have the phone," he said, taking it from her. "I'll navigate." He squinted at the screen for a moment. "It looks like he's driving on a road called West Lake Pass. Shit! You just missed it," he said as she sped past the turnoff.

She braked and turned into a gas station. "*¿Positivo?*" she asked as she swung back around.

"Yeah. Go this way," he replied frantically, waving his hand for her to drive on.

Gauging from the gated driveways, the winding street led through an affluent neighborhood that most likely fronted the lake shore. He checked the phone and saw Becerra was still moving parallel to the lake."

"Wait. It looks like he just turned off of this road and is going towards the lake onto another road. We gotta hurry." He slapped the dash in frustration. "He's getting rid of loose ends, isn't he?"

She didn't reply.

"Give me your knife."

She made a mirthless chortling sound that came out sounding almost like half sob, half amusement.

"*¿Por qué?* You do not trust me? No?"

"No. And I never did. The knife, Vera."

She slowly withdrew the switchblade from her handbag.

"You think I cannot kill you before you can do anything," she said, holding it up in front of her face.

He gripped the Glock he held in his lap. She handed him the knife.

"If you do not trust me, then take it. But remember if there is a chance your woman is still alive, then you will need my help."

"Okay. Keep the goddamn knife. Just remember. You don't kill him until I know where Lilly is. Now we need to figure out where we are. You can do that on this phone, can't you?" he asked, holding the phone up to his face.

She took it from him and studied it as she slowed down. "I think we are very close to where he turned."

Jaime craned his head to try and see if there were any driveways or maybe a road.

"There. You see? I think back there." she said, pointing over her shoulder. She braked and reversed twenty yards or so before swinging the car around to illuminate a break in the thick bank of trees that hugged the sides of the road.

Sure enough Jaime was able to make out a narrow, unmarked, and poorly paved opening almost concealed by overhanging tree branches and waist high weeds.

"You're sure this is where he turned?" she asked.

He looked at the phone again. "Yeah, this is where he turned. It looks like he stopped beside the lake."

Did they dare turn down the road? It couldn't be more than a hundred yards to the lake. Probably less.

"We walk from here. Do you have a flashlight?"

"No, I have only the light on the phone."

"Lets' go," he said, opening the door.

Chapter 32

Lilly estimated it hadn't been no more than five, maybe ten minutes, since they had turned off the dirt road onto a paved street. Occasionally, they passed beneath a street light that allowed Lilly to catch a brief glimpse of the trailer's interior. There appeared to be several small rectangular openings in the ceiling. Ventilation shafts, she guessed. And much too small to crawl through.

Once they slowed to a stop, and the lights from a vehicle behind them sliced through the louvers of more ventilation openings in the rear doors. A minute later, they slowed and she felt them turn off onto a more uneven road surface.

She could hear gravel pinging on the underside of the trailer. The air turned cooler and she could smell the rank scent of decaying vegetation. And then a musty smell that reminded her of the river behind her parents' trailer house in Michigan. Any shred of nostalgia quickly morphed into anxiety. Water. *They were going to dump our bodies in the river.*

"Shit!" She began to chew at the tape around her wrist with renewed motivation. She needed to get loose if they were to have any chance.

After a minute or so, she felt them stop. A moment passed, and she sensed the trailer being turned and then it seemed to be backing up. It stopped, and she heard the slam of a car door closing and voices, but she couldn't make out what they were saying. .

Suddenly, she felt the trailer backing up again. It felt as if they were going down an incline.

Another moment passed, and another door opened and slammed shut. And then came the sound of the bolt on the trailer's doors sliding open. The doors creaked open and the beam of a flashlight allowed Lilly to catch a brief glimpse of the inside of the trailer. She could make out was trampled straw, Jeronimo huddled in the corner, and the silhouette of someone stepping into the trailer.

"*Nosotros estamos aqui,*" Becerra said.

The musty smell of the lake filled her nostrils and she thought she heard the faint lapping of water.

Becerra walked up to them, squatted in front of Jeronimo and shown the flashlight in his face. She saw Jeronimo open his eyes and blink at the light, his face ashen in the glare of the flashlight.

"*¿Sigues vivo, cabron? Bueno,*" Becerra said.

Jeronimo tried to say something in reply but his voice faltered. "*Bastordo,*" she thought he uttered weakly.

She could see now that Becerra held a knife in his hand. He lowered the flashlight, and in one deft swipe, sliced the tape binding Jeronimo's feet. He pivoted and reached for Lilly's feet.

"You know the reason that I do this? Cut your bindings?" he asked as he cut through the tape around her ankles. "So you may be able to stand. It will… *¿Como se dice?* Prolong I believe is the word. It will prolong your deaths."

She tried to kick at him, but her legs were too stiff to move. In desperation, she held out her hands.

"Cut me loose. I dare you," she hissed.

Becerra laughed. "You are brave, but foolish. I will see you both in hell," he said and rose to his feet, He kicked at Jeronimo's legs and then turned and walked out of the trailer.

There came the sound of the bolt sliding shut. A moment of silence followed, and then came a loud banging sound coming from the front of the trailer. And then again, And again. And suddenly the trailer seemed to lurch backwards.

Chapter 33

It now became obvious to her as to what they were doing. The trailer probably sat on some kind of a boat ramp. Becerra meant for the trailer to roll into the lake, she realized as she struggled to her knees, groaning in pain.

"Jeronimo. Do you hear me?"

He muttered something. She half-rolled, half-crawled over to his side.

"We have to get up. Can you stand?"

"I think not."

"You have to, Jeronimo. It's our only chance. Here, I'll help you."

She hooked her arms under his left arm and he winced in pain. "Sorry." She crawled to his other side and hooked her arms under his right arm.

"Okay," she said, struggling to get her knees and feet beneath her stiff legs "On the count of three, I'm going to pull you up. We stand together. *¿Listo? Uno, dos, tres.*"

Jeronimo groaned as she tried lifting him to his feet. He rose to a half-standing position and began to slump back down, but Lilly caught him.

"Come on, *jefe*. You have to stand."

She managed to pull him up into a standing position of sorts just as the trailer shifted and the front tilted upwards, forcing them to flail helplessly in an attempt to keep their footing. She pulled him to his knees.

Then came the sudden sound of water gushing through the louvered ventilation panels at the rear of the trailer.

Mierda. What do we do?" Jeronimo said as he clung to Lilly's arm for support.

"Stay on your feet, *jefe*. It's our only chance. Who knows? The lake may not be that deep. Or maybe we'll just float away."

She could feel the cold water begin to seep through her running shoes. The trailer suddenly began to tilt sideways, and she fought to stay upright while maintaining her grip on Jeronimo's arm.

It was then she felt something sharp dig into her arm. She relaxed her grip on Jeronimo long enough to run her hands against the side of the trailer's wall. There it was - a small shred of jagged metal protruding from the trailer's metal side.

"*Jefe,* I'm going to let you back down. Just for a moment. Don't worry"

She lowered him to the floor and realized the water was already almost a foot deep. Pushing back to her feet, she ran her hands along the wall until she again felt the shard of sharp metal.

It was becoming difficult to maintain her balance on the slick, water-logged and now steeply angled floor. It didn't help that Jeronimo clung tightly to her legs to keep from sliding down into the ever deepening water. She began frantically working the tape that bound her wrists back and forth over the jagged metal.

Chapter 34

The pot-holed pavement gave way to a narrow graveled road lined with dense, waist-high vegetation and overhanging trees. Jaime couldn't be sure where it led although Vera's phone app indicated the road ended at the edge of the lake. He tried to avoid using the light on Vera's phone even though the moonless night and the thick, overhanging trees made it difficult to see.

He had started out in a slow jog, but Vera in her high-heeled sandals had difficulty keeping up in the gravel. He waited for her to catch up.

"If you can't keep up, I'm going ahead."

"I will go barefoot," she replied, leaning on his arm so she could slip off her sandals. "You go," she said, gasping for breath. "Just give me my phone. And promise you will not kill Miguel until I get there."

"I'm not promising anything. Be careful," he said, handing her the phone. "Did you hear that?"

There it was again. A heavy metallic banging sound. Three more bangs followed in quick succession. He was quite sure they weren't gunshots.

"*¿Qué es?*"

"I don't know, but I have to go."

He began to run as fast as he dared on the dark, uneven road. His mind suddenly flashed back to a little over a year ago when he and Lilly had raced through the darkness on a similar road in an attempt to save Jeronimo's granddaughter Kate.

No more of this, he thought bitterly. He promised himself that if he found Lilly, he would, give up this life. He would sell insurance, do data entry, and maybe learn to be a chef, anything but risking his or Lilly's life again.

The road seemed to grow wider and the vegetation less thick. Was he imagining it or did he really see lights up ahead? He stopped to listen. He could hear voices. He took the Glock from his waistband and began walking hurriedly in the direction of the voices.

After thirty yards or so, the roadway suddenly opened onto a clearing. He could see lights from across the lake reflecting off the water's surface, and off to his right, he saw the beams of a couple of flashlights. As he drew nearer, he thought he could see several figures gathered around the lights. There were three, maybe four people at the most, and a pickup truck with its parking lights turned on.

He circled cautiously around the periphery of the opening until he was behind the truck. Further off to the side, parked at the edge of the clearing, he saw what appeared to be a large SUV.

He carefully peered around the side of the truck. Now he could just make out the men silhouetted against the light reflecting off the lake. There were four of them clustered together. Two of then held flashlights. One of them waved his flashlight back and forth across the surface of the lake. The beam of light caught and then settled on the glint of something large and shiny perhaps twenty or thirty yards out into the lake. Whatever it was appeared to be protruding out of the water.

One of the men picked up something from the ground, a large rock perhaps, and hurled it at the object floating on the lake surface. It made a loud, hollow, banging sound, and several of the men laughed. The beam of another flashlight skimmed across the surface and then illuminated the object of their attention.

It took a moment for Jaime to realize what he was seeing, but the shape and what he could see of the sides were unmistakable. He was seeing an enclosed trailer of some sort. It appeared to be half submerged and tilted at an angle. In a flash of recognition, he realized what he was seeing. It was a horse trailer, and his worst instincts told him Lilly was inside.

Chapter 35

It took no more than minute or so for Lilly to saw through the tape and free her hands, although in the process, she lacerated the side of one of her wrists. As she rubbed her numb, blood-soaked hands, she wondered if she could manage to lift Jeronimo to his feet for long enough to cut through his bindings. The water was up to her thighs, and she felt Jeronimo tugging at her waist in an effort to keep from sliding down into the rapidly rising water. She reached down and slid both her hands under his armpits.

"This is going to hurt, *jefe*. But I have to get you up," she said as she tried tugging him to his feet, but he was dead weight. She would have to try loosening the tape binding his wrists by using her fingers and her teeth.

"Leave me, Lilia," he croaked weakly. "Save yourself."

She could barely hear him above the sound of the water gushing into the trailer from all sides.

"Come on *jefe*. Get to your feet. We have to keep our heads above the water."

It was their last and only chance. But for how long? At the rate the trailer was filling up, she figured it would be no more than couple of minutes before their heads would be bobbing against the roof of the trailer.

Suddenly, she heard what sounded like a gunshot. And then another. And people yelling, and the sound of more gunfire.

"*Jefe!* Stand up. Put your arms around my neck and hold on. Come on!"

There was another volley of gunfire, and what she thought sounded like a vehicle driving away. And then silence.

Chapter 36

Jaime realized he had little choice but to open fire on the four men and take his chances. There was no time and little if any likelihood of negotiating surrender. He steadied himself against the side of the truck and began shooting at the silhouettes standing not thirty feet away.

To their misfortune, the four figures had been standing fairly close together. The darkness made it difficult to know for sure, but Jaime felt confident two of the men fell almost immediately. Their flashlights clattered to the ground, and in the fractured beams of light, he saw one of the men disappear into the darkness. A fourth man appeared to drop to his knees and began returning fire, but his shots went wide and slammed harmlessly into the pickup's windshield and grill.

Jaime scrambled away from the truck, took careful aim, and dropped the shooter. Jaime pivoted, crouched down, and peered into the darkness in an effort to locate the fourth man.

There was silence for a long moment, and then he heard what sounded like the door of a vehicle open in the direction of where he thought he had spotted an SUV. There was a flash of light from the SUV's interior dome light and then the sound of the engine starting up. As the headlights flashed on, the SUV accelerated in the direction of the road. Jaime emptied his clip at the fleeing SUV, but was unsure of he had hit anything.

He scrambled over to the three fallen men and scooped up one of the flashlights. It took just a moment to tell that two of the men no longer posed a risk. The third man was crawling away on his stomach. Jaime reached down and pried the man's gun from his hand and tossed it aside. The back of the man's shirt appeared soaked in blood. Jaime rolled him onto his back and lifted him by his shirt.

"Are they in the trailer? *¿Estám en el trailer? Dime!*"

The man stared up at Jaime blankly, blood frothing from his mouth.

Jaime let him drop before scrambling over to the other two men, but it was no use. No one would be talking. He picked up one of the flashlights and shone it out onto the lake. Only the very front of the trailer still protruded above the surface. Every few seconds, large bubbles of air boiled to the surface. There might not be much time before it slid beneath the surface. He quickly kicked off his boots, tossed his gun and the one in his belt onto the ground and dove in.

Chapter 37

When he was just a few strokes from reaching the trailer he heard what sounded like two muffled gunshots in rapid succession, and a few seconds later, another shot. They sounded too faint and far away to be coming from the bank. Then came what sounded like pounding coming from inside the trailer.

"Lilly! Lilly!"

"Jaime!" came the muted response.

"Hang on. I'm coming," he shouted back.

He swam up to the side of the trailer and banged on its side. "Can you hear me?"

"Yeah. Get us out of here. Hurry. Doors in the back."

He took a deep breath and dove. Feeling his way along the side of the trailer, he kicked and pulled himself through the dark water to the rear of the trailer.

He didn't even want to consider the possibility that the doors might be locked or chained shut. If that proved to be the case, he wouldn't have much in the way of options. Running his hands along the rear of the trailer, he finally felt the hasp and then the bolt. He tugged on the bolt, but it wouldn't budge. Out of breath, he kicked back to the surface, took a deep breath, and dove back down. Clutching the bolt with both hands, he twisted it and yanked. To his relief, the bolt slid free. Using his last remaining strength, he pried open the doors. As he did, the trailer suddenly tilted up into an almost vertical position.

Pulling himself inside, he kicked upwards. He felt their legs, and a second later, he broke the surface which was caked with what felt like almost a foot of fetid scum and straw. Raising his hands, he gauged there couldn't be more than a foot of air space remaining in the upended front of the trailer. He reached out in the darkness and touched someone's face. It was Lilly.

"Are you okay?" he asked, gasping for air. He felt someone's arms around her neck.

"Jeronimo. We have to get him out. He's shot," she said with what seemed remarkable calm. "His hands are tied. He won't be able to swim."

"Jeronimo. Can you her me?" Jaime asked, grasping the old man's arm.

"*Si,*" he replied, his voice weak and raspy.

"*Escùchame.* When I tell you to, I want you to take a deep breath and hold it. Then Lilly and I are going to pull you down and out of here. Hold your breath until we're on top. *¿Entender?*"

"*Si.*"

"You ready?" He reached and touched Lilly's face.

"Get me out of here."

"Let's each take one of his arms. We pull him down through the doors and then kick up. Okay? Deep breath. Then…"

There was suddenly a loud thump and the trailer lurched to one side causing them all to momentarily slip below the water. As Jaime broke back through the surface, a large gush of foul air splashed into his face.

"Where is he? Where's Jeronimo?" Lilly shouted as she gasped for air. "I lost him."

A second later, Jeronimo broke through the surface.

"*¿Estás bien?*" she asked, doing her best to keep him from slipping back down.

Si. Okay.*"*

"What happened?" Lilly sputtered.

"I think we hit bottom," Jaime replied, bracing his hands against the roof of the trailer.

"We're almost out of air space." Lilly said, tugging at Jeronimo's arms to prevent him from slipping down and taking her with him.

The doors! A wave of panic swept over Jaime. If the bottom of the trailer had lodged on the lake bottom, the doors might be blocked.

"Hang on. I've gotta check the doors," he said, taking a gulp of the foul air and pushing down.

He momentarily struggled to find his bearings in the dark, muddy water before he found the rear of the trailer. Sure enough one of the doors felt jammed shut, but from what he could tell, the other seemed to be still partially ajar. It would be a tight fit, but he knew they had no other choice but to squeeze their way through the narrow opening. He pushed back up.

"One of them… still open. Part ways." He gasped and took a couple of deep breaths. "We have to go now! I'm going through the door first and I'll pull you through one at a time. Jeronimo. *¿Listo?* Take a deep breath and hang on to Lilly. Here we go!"

It took more effort than he thought to pull Jeronimo down and through the murky water. Once they reached the door, Jaime quickly pushed his way through and waited for what seemed an eternity before feeling Jeronimo wriggle though. Jaime shoved the old man to the surface and reached for Lilly. When he couldn't feel her, he panicked. Where was she? Had she gone back up for air?

Then he felt her arm. He pulled her through and they both kicked their way to the surface. In the darkness, Jaime reached around frantically for Jeronimo.

"Aqui," Jaime heard the old man sputter.

He grabbed Jeronimo by the arm, and began dragging him to the shore. He could hear Lilly splashing behind him. Exhausted, they stumbled ashore and lowered the almost lifeless Jeronimo onto the muddy bank. Lilly collapsed beside him.

"He's… lost a lot of blood," she managed to say between breaths. She pushed herself up to all fours. "You have a knife?"

"No, but hold on."

He scrambled over to one of the men he shot. Turning the dead man over, he jerked a large knife from the man's scabbard and hurried back.

"Let me have it. Your hands are shaking," Lilly said. She proceeded to cut Jeronimo's hands free, and then cut off one of her shirt sleeves. "He needs a hospital," she said, ripping open Jeronimo's shirt.

It was only then that Jaime remembered they had left Vera's truck on the road. And Vera? The gunshots. It had to be Vera. And Becerra? And all she had was her knife.

"Their truck. Maybe they left the keys," Jaime said, retrieving one of the flashlights and hurrying to the truck. To his relief, the keys were still in the ignition. When he returned, Lilly was wrapping the lengthy of sleeve around Jeronimo's shoulder.

"We're in luck. Let's go."

The cool fresh night air and their sudden salvation seemed to have revived Jeronimo to the extent he was able to shuffle between Jaime and Lilly to the truck. It still took considerable effort though to wrestle his dead weight into the front seat. Lilly leaned heavily against the door, seemingly too tired to crawl in beside him.

"How did you find us?" Lilly asked, slumping back against the side of the truck to keep from falling over.

"Vera," he muttered.

"Vera?"

"Becerra's... woman."

"She was with you?"

"I'll explain later. We'd better go."

Lilly straightened up and fell into him. "My leg, it's killing me."

He held her there and felt her shivering, probably from the cold or the terror, or both. He reached up and touched her head, combing the wet tangle of hair from her face. He plucked away something slimy and flicked it away.

"Horse shit," he said.

"No shit." She tried to laugh but ended up choking instead. "But I'm alive. I never…"

"Do you know you're bleeding all over yourself? And me?" he said, shining the light on the front of her shirt.

"My hand. Cut it. Get me out of here."

Jaime hoisted her in beside Jeronimo and walked over to the bank to find his Glock. He paused to shine the light on the dark, calm waters of the lake. There was no sign of the trailer. He shone the flashlight once more on the three dead cartel *pistoleros* and walked back to the truck.

They had driven only a short distance before they saw the red taillights of a vehicle almost blocking the narrow track. It appeared to be a black SUV. Becerra's? As they drew closer, Jaime saw what appeared to be a body lying in the roadway next to the SUV. Jaime pulled up ten feet or so behind it and waited.

"Stay here," Jaime said, retrieving a flashlight and the Glock from the console. He got out and started to chamber a round before remembering he had emptied his only clip at the fleeing SUV.

As he slowly approached the body, Jaime saw the figure on the ground wasn't Vera. Becerra? A pool of blood had soaked into the gravel beneath the man's head. Shards of glass also littered the gravel around his body leaning down; Jaime pulled Becerra onto his back. It appeared as if his throat had been cut. Vera, he thought. He shone the flashlight inside the Escalade. He saw now where the shards of glass had come from. It appeared Becerra had fired a round or two through the driver's side window.

There was no sign of Vera, just lots of blood on the driver's seat. He shone the flashlight in the thick brush on either side of the road, but saw nothing. He waited for a moment before dragging Becerra's body to the side of the road.

"It's Becerra," he said after climbing back into the truck.

Jeronimo raised his head and looked at Jaime. "It is finished then," he muttered. "*Finalizado.*" "

Jaime wondered if that would really prove to be the case. He slipped the truck into gear and managed to find just enough clearance to slip pass the Escalade.

They reached the main road and he saw Vera's truck was gone. He took the flashlight, got out, and retraced his steps to where he thought they had left it. Shining the light on the ground, he immediately spotted the trail of blood leading from the gravel road to where they had parked the truck. She got what she came for, he thought. And quite possibly more. He paused for a moment and then made his way back to the truck.

Chapter 38

Lilly shut her eyes as they wheeled her gurney down the hallway. The bright glare of the overhead lights was making her headache worse. The loud knocking noise inside the CAT machine hadn't helped any either. Nor had the pain medication they had given her soon after they arrived at the emergency room.

Her memory as to how they had reached the hospital was a bit hazy. She vaguely remembered that Jaime pulling outside of some kind of a convenience store. She remembered watching Jaime argue with the store clerk. The young man finally came out from behind the counter and walked out with Jaime into the parking lot. When Jaime opened the pickup truck's door, the clerk cursed and stepped back. She assumed it was the sight of all the blood on the clothes of the two passengers

He ran back inside and must have called the police, ignoring Jaime's demand he call for an ambulance. The police arrived before the ambulance. Since Jaime didn't appear injured, the cops immediately separated Jaime from Lilly and Jeronimo. The last thing she could remember was Jaime being shoved into a patrol car.

The attending doctor at the ER told her she had a probable concussion, and giving in to caution, ordered a CAT scan of her head. After the scan, they brought her back to her bay in the ER where a nurse proceeded to clean her head wound and her lacerated hand.

Somehow she wasn't surprised when the same Fed who had approached her in the park slip through the curtain. Had that only been earlier that day? In her exhaustion and concussed state, she couldn't exactly remember.

"Can you give us a minute?" he asked the nurse as he flashed his badge. He stood there and smiled at Lilly.

"Miss DeFranco. Yeah, I figured you out. You left us enough fingerprints."

"You mind if I see your ID?" she asked him.

He took his wallet from his pants pocket, opened it, and held it out to her.

"You'd better read it to me. I'm not seeing so well."

"Walter Freeman, FBI Special Agent. I'm with the Drug Task Force," he said, pulling up a chair.

"Before you sit, would you mind handing me my water glass? And that ice pack. And if you don't mind, ask them if they can dim those fucking lights?"

He handed her the ice pack and held her glass for her as she sucked down half of it from the straw.

"The lights. I don't know," he said, looking around the room. "I actually prefer them bright when I do interrogations," he said with a grin,

"Is that what this is? Do I need a lawyer?" she asked, clasping the ice pack to her swollen eye.

"Depends," he replied, settling into the chair. "You know you have a rather impressive resume. Fifty pages in fact."

When she didn't say anything, he pulled a small notebook from his shirt pocket and, then hesitated for a moment before placing it back into his pocket.

"But I'm not here to make any new entries." He studied her for a moment. "You don't look anything like your photo from Perryville."

She held to her silence, and he only nodded as if contemplating something.

"You'll be surprised to know that I was able to track down this guy with the unlikely name of Davey Crockett. You remember him, don't you? The ATF guy. He sure remembers you. He wanted me to extend his congratulations."

"Congratulations? For what?"

"I'm guessing he was surprised you managed to stay alive. When you dropped off the radar, in Mexico, he assumed the cartel finally caught up with you."

She allowed herself a smile. She wanted to say that she had caught up with the cartel instead, but decided there wasn't any point in padding her resume.

"Davey Crockett," she muttered. "I never thought I'd hear from him again."

"You'll be happy to know he's a man of his word. That's the only reason that as soon as they discharge you, you're free to go. No questions asked."

"You don't want to know what happened."

"Your friend Soledad filled us in with most of what happened after the shootout at the hotel. Just for the record, tell me something. Did you shoot the guy back at the hotel?"

"I might have. It also could've been friendly fire. I can't swear to anything. This concussion, you know."

"Anyway, we're figuring that you and Soledad did us a favor. A few less cartel assholes to deal with. Don't expect a medal or any fancy citation though."

"Where's Jaime?"

"He'll be waiting for you. There's really nothing we feel inclined to charge him with."

"And Jeronimo?"

"Same goes for him. He's still in surgery. He may have to spend a couple of days here before he's able to travel. It might be a bit longer for this Ernesto guy. Yeah, he made it, too. He's in ICU though. Tough old bastard. The bunch of you earned get out of jail free cards. It seems some federal prosecutor in Mexico City cut some kind of a deal with somebody in DC. Your boss must have friends in high places," Freeman said, pushing to his feet.

"Wait a minute. What happened to the woman? The hitter? Vera?"

He considered his reply for a moment and the shrugged. "She's either in the wind or she crawled off into some hole to die. The cops found a pickup abandoned at a mall parking lot near here. There was quite bit of blood in the driver's seat. The fingerprints we found match those they sent us from Mexico."

"You know she probably killed Becerra."

Freeman nodded. "Soledad told us that he thinks her reason for being here was to take him out on the orders of someone in Jalisco. The prosecutor in Mexico City told us that this Vera and Becerra had once been an item. They think she had done quite a few jobs for Becerra. And maybe the Jalisco, too. It seems she was bit of the wild card in all this. What did Soledad call her? *La carta aùn no jimgada.* The card not yet played. Yeah, *yo hablo español.* I have to speak Spanish in this job."

"You've got this all figured out?"

"Not entirely. There's the possibility that she was supposed to take out your boss, too. And tie up any loose ends while she was at it. You guys were lucky." He started for the door, but turned back around. "It seems you've led a rather charmed life, Miss DeFranco."

"It's Montez, Lilia Montez."

He nodded. "Well, Miss Montez. I hope your luck holds," he said and walked out.

A few minutes passed before one of the nurses came back in.

"The doc's going to come soon and sew up your hand."

"Is there any chance I could get a shower first? I still smell like horse shit."

"I'll see what I can do," she replied and started to walk out.

"Hold on. Do you think the doctor would mind ordering another test? I can give you a urine sample."

"If you're worried about a bruised kidney, there wasn't any blood in the sample you already gave us. You're fine. Is there something else you want checked in your urine? Drug test, maybe? Oh," she added with a smile. "Something else. I'll bring you a cup."

Chapter 39
MEXICO CITY
ONE MONTH LATER

Hilario slowed as he pulled into Jeronimo's drive. There were half a dozen cars parked along the curb that edged the expansive lawn – two were large SUVs, the rest newer model Mercedes sedans. Lilly noted one of the SUVs bore a government license plate.

Several men, some in chauffeurs' uniforms, stood smoking cigarettes alongside a large black SUV. As Hilario edged the car past them, he raised one bony finger in greeting.

¿Qué está pasando aqui?" Lilly asked, leaning over the front seat.

Hilario shrugged. *"No sé. Tal vez, una fiesta?"*

That was odd. Jeronimo hadn't mentioned anything about a party. He just said he wanted her and Jaime to come by to discuss some business. She clicked her tongue in irritation.

Why hadn't he said anything about having guests? Maybe she misheard Jeronimo's directive about arriving at three.

She wasn't dressed for any kind of a social gathering. Just before leaving her apartment, she had changed out of her workout clothes and into a pair of rumpled linen slacks and a designer T-shirt, albeit one with an embroidery calla lily on one sleeve. Street chic perhaps, but it still wasn't suitable for a party.

Hilario guided the Mercedes past the cars and up the drive before beginning his usual, painstakingly slow routine of turning off the ignition and adjusting the mirror to nod to Lilly to acknowledge of their arrival before

He opened her door, extended his hand, and gently helped her out of the car.

"*Pequeña madre,*" he croaked.

Little mother? Lilly shook her head. There was no sense admonishing him even though his endearment had preceded any obvious outward sign of her pregnancy. She was a mere two months in.

Jeronimo vehemently denied disclosing her condition to anyone other than Maria, his housekeeper who herself was pregnant.

"These *Indios,*" Jeronimo tried to explain. "*Ellos son místicos.*"

"Mystical, my ass. Maria must've told Hilario," had been her rejoinder.

"*Gracias,* Hilario," she said and curtsied.

As she started up the walkway, she spotted Jaime and Alphonso, Jeronimo's grizzled, elderly doorman, standing on the steps.

"Did I miss something?" she asked Jaime as she started up the short flight of stairs to the portico. "Or are we early?"

Jaime shrugged. "Alphonso says there's some meeting that's running late," he replied, taking her hand as if to guide her up the steps.

She pulled her hand away. Everyone was suddenly treating her differently, as if she were fragile, not merely knocked up.

Jaime pulled her close and gave her peck on the lips. "How are you feeling?"

"Jesus, I'm fine." She stepped back and smiled. "Did all my puking this morning wake you up?"

"I read somewhere once that vomiting in the morning is a good sign. If you're pregnant, that is."

She turned and nodded at Alphonso.

"*Buenas tardes, Alphonso.*"

"*Buenas tardes, Señorita Montez,*" he replied with a broad smile.

It was good to have Alphonso back. Some three months ago, he had been replaced by two young men dressed in suits and sporting ear pieces and Uzis. At the time, Jeronimo had been preparing for the possibility of a hostile takeover at the hands of one the cartels. Lilly could only assume that the return to the status quo signaled an accord had reached between Jeronimo and one or both of the two cartels that were seeking to secure supremacy in Mexico City's criminal underworld.

Despite the fact that Jeronimo no longer represented any significant factor in this struggle, the cartels still offered him at least a formal nod of regard if for no reason than Jeronimo's far-reaching political connections. Still, he was far from being even remotely considered an elder statesman for he had always openly condemned the cartels for their drug trafficking. He considered their involvement in drugs and prostitution as loathsome and beneath him. Surely not worth the time or effort compared to the relatively more respectable and staid pursuit of simple graft in the form of protection rackets, illegal gambling, bribery, and influence peddling.

"I guess we can wait," Jaime said, motioning to a pair of deck chairs.

"Any idea what this us about?" she asked, settling into one of the chairs.

"Well, I haven't given him my letter of resignation yet. Maybe he just wants to amend the Human Resources handbook to cover maternity leave," Jaime said with a smirk.

Before she could reply, the front door opened and two well dressed, older men stepped out and started down the walkway. A moment later, four others followed. The last group seemed engrossed in a serious conversation, the gist of which Lilly couldn't make out. After making their way down the sidewalk, they said their goodbyes and went to their respective vehicles.

"Interesting," Lilly said. "I recognized the last guy. I've seen him on TV. He's some politician. I think."

"Yeah, he's a cabinet minister. Of exactly what, I'm not sure."

"And the other ones?"

"I'm pretty sure one of them used to the Deputy Police Chief. This should make for some interesting conversation." He glanced at his watch. "He said three. Let's not keep him waiting. We don't want to give him enough time to make up any stories."

Maria met them at the front door and offered Lilly a conspirator smile. The way everyone treated her was becoming irksome, Lilly thought as she followed Maria down the long hallway to Jeronimo's office. She paused momentarily to offer Bruno the macaw a peanut before catching up to Jaime. Maria knocked before opening the door and motioned them inside.

Jeronimo sat his desk, his attention focused on the screen of his computer. He paid their entrance little heed for perhaps a half minute before looking up at them. The sling his doctor had ordered him to wear for his injured shoulder hung loosely on the back of his chair. He had undergone two separate surgeries for his shattered left shoulder, one in Austin, and the other here in Mexico City. He still appeared wan and far from fully recovered from his gunshot wound or the trauma of almost drowning in that horse trailer.

"You are well?" he asked Lilly.

"Christ, I wish all of you would just stop it," she said, not bothering to conceal her annoyance.

Jeronimo appeared to be suitably penitent for he held up his hand as if in apology. "Please. Sit," he said, motioning to both of them to take seat. "Something to drink? A bit to eat? *Un refrigerio?*"

"Maybe some green tea," Lilly replied.

"Nothing for me," Jaime said, settling in beside Lilly.

Jeronimo nodded, rose, and stepped out of the office to instruct Maria. His gait appeared stiff. It was apparent to both Lilly and Jaime that the past several weeks had aged him.

"Are you still going to tell him today that you're quitting?" Lilly asked.

Before Jaime could reply, Jeronimo came back and took his place behind the desk.

"I apologize for keeping you waiting. It could not be helped." He cleared his throat. "You may have noticed the gentlemen that have just left. Some of whom are business associates. Perhaps you recognized a certain government official or two with whom I have had a long standing relationship. I felt I owed them an explanation for what I am about to undertake."

Jaime shot a questioning glance at Lilly who offered a slight shrug.

"You have both been aware that I have been divesting myself from any activities that might be deemed… Very well, I shall say it. Criminal in nature. As of today, I have ended any involvement in such activities. This has proven to be rather complicated, but it will be completed after my meeting later with my attorney."

"Does this have anything to do with the cartels pressuring you?" Lilly asked.

"Ah, Lilia. As always you come directly to the point," he replied. "One of your admirable traits." He hesitated and sighed. "I believe you are both aware of my connection with a certain individual in the Jalisco cartel. This person has intimated that the Vera woman had been tasked with eliminating Becerra. If my efforts to have the Americana authorities deal with him failed, then she was to serve as the fall back option. I have since also discovered that I was indeed the secondary target."

"The card not played," Lilly murmured. "So now what? A truce?"

"Of sorts. It is only a matter of time before they attempt to take over my operations. If not Jalisco, then the Sinaloa. I fear it is inevitable and I wish to forego any… violence. Regardless, I have done my best to divest myself from any association with … these people."

"I'm curious, *jefe*," Jaime interjected. "Did your Jalisco source have anything to say about what happened to Vera?"

Jeronimo shook his head. "No. And I asked, but he would not say. Before I was discharged from the hospital in Austin the American agent visited me. I asked him this very same thing and all he said was that they believe from the amount of blood in her vehicle that it was unlikely she survived. Then again, she may have had resources."

"Let's just hope we don't have to be looking over our shoulders," Jaime said.

"I believe that is unlikely. Nevertheless, let us return to the reason I summoned you." He cleared his throat again. "I find myself fortunate to have accrued considerable wealth. My father left me a great deal of money and properties. I have managed to build on that wealth. Not in the ways my father would've approved, but nevertheless, I am a wealthy man."

He paused as if collecting his thoughts. "It is time to make certain arrangements. I will come to the point. Jaime," he said, directing his gaze at Jaime. "I am appointing you as the manager overseeing my investments and my properties. I have already appointed a board of directors to assist you in this."

Jaime shook his head in surprise. "Boss, I'm not a businessman. There's no way I…"

Jeronimo raised his hands to stop him. "There is no one I trust more. I am confident you will… grow into these responsibilities." He turned his gaze to Lilly. "And you, *chica.* You have proven your loyalty beyond measure. I have set aside a considerable amount of my fortune to be placed in a charitable trust that you will mange as you see fit."

Lilly sat there in stunned silence, at a loss for words. Before either of them could say anything, he went on. "I have gone to great lengths to ensure that my more valued associates and employees have been compensated for their service."

"And you?" Lilly managed to finally ask. "You don't seem to be the type to just sit around. What are going to do all day? Water your orchids?" she asked, nodding at the large glassed in solarium behind him.

"Hattie has invited me to Houston to stay with her for a while. I believe she means to rehabilitate me," he said with a smirk.

Hattie was Kate's grandmother and at one time Jeronimo's lover and apparently the thief of his heart. She was now a Buddhist nun who ran a halfway house for women in Houston.

Lilly and Jaime exchanged glances and smiled. They had both seen how the two of them interacted when Hattie had come to visit Kate. Buddha be damned. The embers still seemed to be smoldering.

"You will both serve as the executors of a trust I have established in Kate's name. She is still quite young and impetuous. I leave it to you both to decide when she is capable of responsibly managing her own affairs. There is one other detail that must be discussed," he said, offering a rare smile. "The wedding."

"The wedding? You mean you and Hattie are finally getting real?" Lilly asked.

"You know what I mean. I intend for it to take place here. And by the way, this house is much too large for just me. I expect you to move in here. It has been too long since there was any joy in this house."

"I don't know what to say," Jaime said. "You are too generous. As far as a wedding goes, we haven't made any plans."

"Then do it. It is my final order." He glanced at this watch, "I apologize for leaving so abruptly, but I have details I still need to complete. We will have dinner later and discuss the plans."

He rose to his feet, placed his hand over his mouth and hurried out.

"Jesus," Lilly said after a moment of stunned silence. "I didn't see this coming."

"Yeah," was all Jaime could manage.

Lilly scooted closer to Jaime. "I guess we've got some plans to make."

"I guess so. Are you wondering where I went this morning?" he asked.

"Tell me. Shopping for rings maybe?"

His face grew somber. "Jeronimo doesn't know but I met with his contact inside Jalisco."

She pulled back. "You're kidding. Why?"

"Vera."

"He told us she's most likely dead, but I didn't buy it. It seems they don't want to talk about it. Here's the thing. A couple of weeks ago when I was in Guadalajara, I saw an article in the Guadalajara newspaper. It said that a ten year old girl was reportedly abducted from a convent outside of the city. And there's been no trace of her since."

"What are you saying? That maybe Vera was telling the truth about having a kid?"

He shrugged. "Who knows?"

Neither of them said anything for a moment. "Do you really think the cartel will leave Jeronimo alone? Leave us alone?" she asked.

"We'll just have to see." He looked at his watch. "We've got time to go somewhere for coffee. We can talk about the wedding."

"Is that your punk ass way of proposing? You knock me up and then you ask?"

"Are you having second thoughts?"

"No. Are you?"

"I gotta admit to being scared. About a wedding, not so much. It's you who scares me."

"Good. Best you always keep that in mind."

He took her face in his hands and kissed her. "I'll go have Hilario bring the car around."

"You do that, *güero.*"

She watched him walk out as she shook her head in wonderment. Another card played. Not even three years ago, she had been five years into a fifteen year prison sentence, and yet here she was. Soon to be married and a mother to boot.

She thought of Harlan Quist and something he had once told her about redemption not having to be perfect. And that it was all about remembrance of the past and forgiving oneself. Would it really be that simple? She certainly hoped so.

She left the office and stepped out onto the porch to wait. It had rained while they were inside and now a rainbow arched over the Bosque de Chapultepec. The air smelled of wet grass and pines. And promise.

Alphonso rose to his feet and nodded at the sky. "*Una tarde maravillosa. ¿ sr?*"

She placed her one hand on her stomach.

"*Si. Muy maravililosa.*"

She patted his shoulder and walked down the steps.

THE END

Author website- dennisjung.com